T0196538

Trust Fall

Trust Fall

A NOVEL BY

PATRICK ROONEY

iUniverse, Inc.
Bloomington

Trust Fall

iUniverse books may be ordered through booksellers or by contacting:

iUniverse
1663 Liberty Drive
Bloomington, IN 47403
www.iuniverse.com
1-800-Authors (1-800-288-4677)

Cover design and image ©2012 Sarah E Melville, Sleeping Basilisk Design

ISBN: 978-1-4759-0718-6 (sc)
ISBN: 978-1-4759-0719-3 (hc)
ISBN: 978-1-4759-0720-9 (ebk)

Printed in the United States of America

iUniverse rev. date: 04/02/2012

For my family, caricatured

but never unloved.

PART 1

"You, you, you, you," she said. "You're my fondest wish, Roland. You're my *only* wish. You and you, forever and ever."

-Stephen King
Wizard and Glass

Chapter 1

Joe woke from a stuffy sleep to hear heavy footsteps in the hall. His loins were tender. As always, it took a half second for Joe to realize where he was. He was in his bedroom at his dad's house. His father's footsteps triggered mild dread—combined this morning with a vague anxiety that he had been caught sneaking out. He glanced at the window by his bed, double-checking that he had replaced the screen. Joe always used his window as an exit in his rendezvous with Vanessa because it was quieter than the heavy front door.

A knock fell twice on the door before it swung open without waiting for a reply. This was invariably how Joe's father entered Joe's room.

"It's noon," said Ralph King, looking down at his son, tangled in the sheets. "Go mow the lawn." The dogs ran in and leaped on Joe's bed, clambering all over him and licking at his head and face.

"Opal, Ebony! Get down!" (Joe's stepmother, whose hobby was decorating, had named the dogs.) Yelling at the dogs being in vain, Joe shoved them off the bed, moving awkwardly in fear that his boxers had shifted in his sleep. He felt uncomfortable about his dad seeing his junk.

But Ralph King just smirked maddeningly. "Go mow the lawn," he said again. "I've let you sleep half the day and you need to contribute to this family. If I can provide for your food and clothing you can—"

"Dad, okay!" Joe said. "I'll mow the lawn."

His dad eyed him. Joe had been taller than him since seventh grade. Ralph King had short brown hair and a short brown goatee.

"Watch your tone." He left without closing the door.

Joe padded down the aggregate hallway which gnawed at his bare feet and went into the bathroom. He looked at his reflection in the mirror, which was blurry because he wasn't wearing his glasses or contacts. He was tall and thin. His dirty-blond hair was long enough to cover the tips of his ears. He was clean-shaven except for the hair he allowed to grow on his chin.

Joe reached in the shower and turned the water on.

"Joe!" his dad shouted from outside the bathroom door. "I told you to mow the lawn!"

"I was just going to shower first!" Joe protested. He heard the whining in his own voice and hated it.

"Joe, you idiot! Take a shower *after* you mow the lawn. Otherwise you'll get dirty again right after you've showered!"

In the past Joe had argued that he didn't get that dirty mowing the lawn. But that really wasn't the point. The point was that showering *after* mowing the lawn was the way that Ralph King thought the universe was supposed to align. It was this same principle that made Mr. King so irritated when someone sat at the table with a plastic drinking glass when everyone else at the table had a glass one. For that matter, it was the same principle that led him to hate chewing gum ("tacky") and to believe that his offspring should wash his car every weekend.

Joe liked to shower in the morning to help himself fully wake up. And this morning he was anxious to shower because he thought he might still smell a little like sex.

"NOW!" Joe's dad yelled.

"Okay, okay!" Joe tried to feel that he was too happy, everything considered, to let his dad's lack of respect get to him, but the more he and Vanessa made love, the less this worked. The newness was wearing off.

Not that he was complaining.

2

Joe called Vanessa that night, as he did every night. She answered the phone by saying, "I love you," in her sweetest voice.

"I love you, too," Joe smiled. He paced his bedroom as he spoke, out of habit.

"Last night was amazing. As always."

"Yeah," Joe said. "It was."

"I love being intimate with you."

He lay back on his bed. He looked around his room, not consciously seeing anything. His gray matter took in the familiar images of Joe's Room At Dad's House. He had a desk, a TV, and a small bookshelf, though he kept most of his books at his mom's house—HOME, according to the gray matter. He had a picture on his desk of himself and Vanessa dressed up for the school's Winter Formal. His dad bought him a suit for the occasion and she wore a pretty black and pink dress. He had band posters: Blindside (signed) and the Red Hot Chili Peppers. He also had a twelve-month calendar with pictures of cats doing funny things (a gift from his aunt), and a small portrait of Jesus, his eyes gazing heavenward. It was of some sort of foil material, so that the colors gleamed in a stained glass kind of effect. "Very . . . Catholic," his youth pastor had said when he bought it during a trip to Mexico.

"I watched the news tonight. Got a biting myspace blog out of it."

"Oh yeah," said Vanessa. "I saw that."

"What did you think?"

"I dunno." Joe could almost see her shrug. "I mean, I don't really care about politics."

"What? Since when?"

"Well, I care about important things. Just not about some random person and what they did."

"You mean Alberto Gonzales."

"Yeah, whoever." Vanessa laughed.

The gray matter that made its dwelling between Joe's ears whispered that if Joe wanted to avoid an argument, now was the time to drop the subject. Joe ignored this voice.

"Well, the attorney general has a pretty important position. John Ashcroft was pretty influential, and it's good to be rid of him. But at the same time, Alberto Gonzales, the new guy, wants to torture people. It's all important stuff."

There was a pause.

"I guess I'm just stupid, then," Vanessa said.

"You're not stupid, Vanessa."

"Well, obviously I am, since I don't even know who Alberto whoever is."

"Hey. You are not stupid," Joe said. "Listen, forget about it. I'm sorry. I love you. You're everything to me. We're gonna get married."

A pause.

"Vanessa?"

"Say all that again."

He did. Later, they prayed together before saying goodnight.

These two sexually infatuated teens praying together may seem inconsistent. Nor was this some new wave kind of faith they practiced. It was old-fashioned evangelical Protestantism.

Joe was the more devout of the two, and had encouraged Vanessa to start going to youth group in the first place. She said now and then that without him, she wouldn't have gotten close to God again.

All this religion was enough to make them feel it was necessary to rationalize having sex. Therefore they were the five hundred seventy-three billionth young Christian couple over the ages to feel that it was okay because they were going to get married one day. This perspective is more relaxed than the Not Until The First Night Of Your Honeymoon school of thought, but more uptight than those holding to the It's Okay If You're In Love way of thinking. The If It Feels Good Do It contingency is a horse of an entirely different color, and Joe thought of those flushed and sticky souls with pity and envy.

Joe prayed before every meal, before going to sleep, and with Vanessa every night. He went to Auberry Community Church Youth Group every week, and to church on the Sundays he was at his mom's house. He read four chapters of his Bible every day, and meditated on them. If you were to look inside Joe's secret heart, you would find that God was the most important thing to him. In Vanessa's, in spite of her best efforts, you would find Joe King.

Chapter 2

It was the last week of school before summer. Joe went to Sierra High in the foothills where he lived with his mother. Driving from Fresno to the nearest district bus stop wasn't much fun. He wasn't a morning person, and was less prepared to deal with his father's lectures and haranguing. Even Ralph King's sense of humor involved unrelenting banter and verbal sparring. He also hated it when Joe slouched in the passenger seat. Slouching wasn't part of Ralph King's view of how the universe should align.

At school Joe followed the same basic pattern he'd followed for two years. His eyes took in the mountains that flanked the school, dead grass coloring them tawny in the summer's growing heat, with patches of gray granite. "**05**" shone out on a large rock in rectangular spray-painted digits. Next year's seniors would soon change it to "**06**."

The June day flew by. Joe found himself in his sixth period class, Honors World Cultures. Miss Edaus taught the class, a young, quirky woman (read: hot). This opinion merited discussion with two guys who sat near him. Eddie tended to agree, while Hank favored Miss Peach the science teacher, and her glorious bosom. Joe's interactions with the two were mostly limited to class time, mostly because neither of them was Vanessa Grey. Her assigned seat was on the other side of the room.

They talked about comic books. Joe wasn't well versed in the subject. Hank and Eddie were enlightening him.

"That's the Punisher," Hank in concluded. "That's the Punisher in a nutshell. Hey," he said abruptly. "Did I ever tell you guys that I named my penis?"

He hadn't.

"My penis is named the Punisher."

"Mine's the Unstoppable Juggernaut," said Eddie.

Vanessa left class first. He called to her and she turned to reveal a stony expression. Her dark eyes looked out above her Roman nose. Vanessa hated that nose, but Joe always reassured her with complete honesty that he loved it.

"What's the matter?"

She exhaled an almost-laugh. "Well," she said, "you just completely ignored me back there in class."

"I wasn't ignoring you, I was just talking to Hank and Eddie."

"While I was all alone." Sunlight shone on them through gaps in a vine-covered chain-link fence. Students on their way to class glanced at them, a bell rang and Joe felt conspicuous. He didn't know what to say, but he knew by now that relationships weren't all I love yous and orgasms.

"You were welcome to join us," he said.

She sighed. "They don't like me."

"What? Sure they do—what makes you think that?"

"I can tell when people don't like me."

"I think they like you fine, Butterfly," said Joe. "What's not to like?"

"Hmm."

"Anyway, we spend every break and lunch together—which I love—is it so bad that I was talking to other people in class?"

"Yeah but in just three days in will be summer, and I'll never get to see you." Her voice rose an octave.

"That's not true. We'll still see each other at summer school, and at youth group." He didn't mention how little he was looking forward to school during the summer.

Even as she protested he could see she was warming to him. It was in her stance, which no longer telegraphed "fuck you," but something more akin to "I'm stressed. Hold me."

"Yeah, but that's not as much as when school's in. I just wanted to enjoy being with you now while we can spend time together."

"Okay. You're right." He hugged her, kissed her lips. They tasted sweet, like a brand new orange plucked and peeled.

2

That night Joe lay in bed at his mom's house. He looked at the glow-in-the-dark stars his stepbrother pasted on the ceiling when it was his room, way back when. Andrew arranged some of the stars on the ceiling fan so that it made a spiral when it was turned on. It looked like a black hole.

Sleep was slow coming to Joe. He thought about when he and Vanessa had just fallen in love, many months ago now. He remembered those early conversations, the first impassioned declarations of love, over the telephone or typed on a glowing computer screen in the dark when the house was asleep. He'd been fortunate to fall in love with his soulmate the first time he'd been in love with anybody.

"We'll always be together," he'd said. "For our entire lives and afterwards—we'll be together in heaven." Joe melted when Vanessa whispered, "I love you," into his ear.

"I love you too. My everything. My Butterfly."

3

He enjoyed two weeks of swimming in the pool and eating popsicles by the carton in the heat waves baking up from the concrete—and then there he was, in a desk once again—and at his old middle school, no less.

Summer school began two weeks after school got out. Mercifully, it was only four half-days a week, ending around noon. It lasted for six of their ten weeks of vacation. Joe and Vanessa were both taking summer school to "get some classes out of the way"—to clear their schedules for their Junior and Senior years. That was the idea, anyway.

On the first day of class, Joe looked around the room at the people he knew and didn't know. There was Nathan Licht, who was Peter Sandstrom's cousin. Joe still considered Peter his best guy friend even though he hadn't hung out with him on a regular basis since going out with Vanessa. Joe had been to Nathan's house once or twice. There was Justin Neil, who Joe had been friends with in elementary school years. He had moved away from the school district for a few years to join a foster home, then had come back as a different person; a goth-metal badass with waist-length hair dyed black.

There were more than a few kids who seemed young to him—incoming freshmen. One was a heavyset blond girl who would place London on the continent of Africa during a map exercise. Mr. Rolsten was telling the class they'd have S.S.R. for the first ten minutes of class every morning (Joe hadn't had "Silent Sustained Reading" in class since middle school), when Kay Robideau walked into class. Joe knew her from band and German. She was talkative, enthusiastic, intelligent (unlike, to tell the truth, Nathan Licht and Justin Neil), a little bit melodramatic and often cheerfully misanthropic, swore a lot, and above all loathed George

W. Bush. Perhaps, in their conservative bubble of a community, this was what Joe liked most of all about her.

After the 2004 election, Kay made a huge paper banner reading, "George W. Bush—NOT my president." She'd shown it to Joe in German class, and he'd added his signature to it. Then she'd put it up on the free speech board by the quad at break, where it was torn down by noon.

She sat next to Joe, to his mild surprise. "Hey Joe," she said. "Hey Eva," she said to a Hispanic girl ahead of her.

They'd started on some map worksheets Mr. Rolsten had passed out when Kay suddenly laughed.

"What?" Joe asked.

"Um," Kay said. "Okay—just say something weird. Anything at all."

"Cauliflowers kill infants," Joe said.

"*What* did you say? Oh—I get it—you're just *Joe-King!*" Kay said, tapping his name on the worksheet. She uttered an overzealous laugh. "I'm sorry—people probably say that all the time."

Geography was easy, so Joe had plenty of opportunities to gab with Kay.

"The kids in our class who were going to Germany are gone now," she said one day. If you had taken at least two years of German, you could go to Germany for four weeks during the summer with Frau Lismore and live with a host family. Both Joe and Kay had been eligible to go on the trip, which wasn't made every year, and Joe hadn't told anyone the real reason he had passed it up. Whenever he'd mentioned the trip, using phrases like "once in a lifetime chance," Vanessa had come back with "It seems like everybody is always leaving me behind," or "don't forget me while you're there."

In the end he decided not to go. Vanessa's surprise surprised him. Hadn't she known he would give things up for her? He told her they would tour Europe together one day, and soon after she suggested he take summer school, since she would be. They'd get to see each other that way, she said.

"Oh yeah," Joe said.

"It kind of bothers me," Kay continued. "The only reason I didn't go to Germany was because my boyfriend was all, 'Oh, Kay, I really want to spend time with you this summer,' but he's been so busy that I haven't even seen him at all."

"Huh," Joe said. "Well . . ." so Kay became the first person that Joe did tell.

Joe held no grudge against his girlfriend for any of it and soon he and Kay and Eva met Vanessa for lunch, eating at the outside tables the cool kids had occupied when they'd attended Foothill Middle School. Associating with mostly girls was nothing new to Joe.

There were bright sides to the merciless hundred-degree-plus weather and they were bent into curvy cylinders—Vanessa's legs exposed by her short shorts. She'd giggle when she hugged Joe and half the time felt his erection pressing into her thigh. It was starting to be a while since they'd had the chance to fool around. Joe would find himself expressing willingness to go to his dad's house, because Vanessa was saying her parents were *maybe thinking about* going to spend the night at her grandma's house. But somehow it kept not happening.

"I can't wait 'till tomorrow," Vanessa told Joe over her PB&J sandwich while everybody else around them talked to everybody else.

Tomorrow would be their one-year "anniversary."

Chapter 3

They went to a pond near Vanessa's house to celebrate. They had it all to themselves. Joe's mom drove them to Vanessa's house, picking her up before driving the short distance to the lake, where they unloaded Vanessa's plastic kayak and some sodas. Normally, Vanessa's parents were maniacally paranoid about the two of them being alone together. Joe believed her mother had estimated the amount of time it would take him to impregnate Vanessa and placed any time above forty-five seconds squarely in the danger zone. But it had all worked out. Vanessa's stepfather was out of town for a few days, working on a construction project, and her mother was too doped up on pills for back pain to protest (the more Vanessa told Joe about her mom, the more he suspected that she had more than a strictly needs-based relationship with Vicodin).

Joe waited until his mom drove away, then reached for Vanessa's hips, pulling her in for a kiss.

"Happy anniversary," he said. Her hair swung against his shoulders, and she grinned the grin that always withered him—the grin that she did with her teeth and her eyes and her whole face.

"Happy anniversary. I love you."

She lived a little ways up the mountains in a place called Meadow Lakes. This was the lake the moniker promised. Perhaps Meadow Ponds didn't have the same ring. Surrounded by green and the smell of pine, they dragged the kayak through seaweedy plants growing near the shore and slipped in. Vanessa leaned forward to kiss Joe again and then they sat back facing each other, watching the way the sun dappled and played on their skin and clothes as Joe rowed them slowly and aimlessly toward the center of the almost-lake. It was fine to be in love and to feel the rhythm of the paddle as one end, then the other dipped placidly into the water with a quiet splash and spiraling ripples.

"When do you think we should get married?" Joe asked. It wasn't the first time the subject had been broached.

"I don't know," Vanessa said slowly. She looked up at him and smiled. Joe felt her love for him as powerfully as though it were a physical thing—a blanket she'd thrown on him. "I feel like we're already married, you know? We love each other, and we're together. Who cares about the ceremony of the thing?"

"I know. I feel the same way." Near them, a mother duck paddled ahead of her ducklings, lined up single file. It would take a truly soulless person to not grin at the yellow puffs bumbling along after their saintly and dignified guardian. "I do want to get married one day, though."

"Me too."

"My parents would have a fit if we did it right after high school." Nothing was simple. "On the other hand, they'd be equally outraged by us living together during college, not married. And we're pretty much planning on that, aren't we?"

"Well, I thought so."

"Good, good. I want to. I know it will be hard to go against my parents, but it's worth it. You're worth it."

Vanessa sighed. Our parents just have to learn that our lives are ours, not theirs."

"My dad and my stepmom would definitely prefer us living together than getting married. They'd think it'd be a huge mistake to get married so young. My—"

"I hate that. What does age have to do with it?" We love each other, and we're mature."

"Well, right. It's ageism, is all—it's discrimination, you know? Think that Romeo and Juliet were younger than we are." He paddled. A heavy bank of gray clouds began to drift toward the sky above them. "Anyway, but of course Tobias and my mom would be dead set against living together without us being married. It's hard. I don't know what to do."

"Well, what do *you* want?" Vanessa asked.

"To marry you as soon as possible."

"Okay," she said. "Well then that's what we'll do." She leaned forward again to kiss him, pressing her palms to the sides of his face so her fingers forked at his earlobes. The kayak wobbled, but kept holding them upright.

"It is hard, though, you know," Joe said, dreading what his parents' reaction would be.

"I know, baby," she said. "But I love you."

"I know you do," Joe said. "And I love you too."

He thought of his family's upcoming trip to the coast—Spirit West Coast, a Christian music festival. He'd invited her, but she hadn't bothered to ask and be forbidden to go by her parents. He needed to tell her it was coming up, but didn't want to just then, or that day.

"Why don't you paddle us to dry land?" she broke into his thoughts. "We probably have just an hour or so to enjoy our special day before a parental comes back."

"Why don't we rock the boat a little instead?"

"I don't think it'll work in this thing," she replied. "It's not exactly a cruise liner."

"Oh, alright." Tomorrow, he thought. I'll tell her tomorrow.

2

It was a mess of horns and flippy guitar—a hyperactive symphony of sincerity and rebellion. It was beautiful, was what Joe was trying to say.

"Forever indebted to you," he said to Eva again.

"I'm glad you like it," she said. "I love introducing people to great music. It's my favorite thing."

"I love it," Joe said again. She laughed.

"I've never met a trumpet player who didn't love ska." She got a look in her eye, then—and asked with the passion of a missionary: "I really want to start a ska band. Would you want to be in it?"

"Um—yeah! That would be awesome."

"Great! I was thinking Kay could play saxophone, I'm gonna play guitar—we'll figure it all out."

"I can't wait."

"A *ska band*?" Vanessa asked, not two hours later. She leaned with her back against his chest and he could feel her words vibrate against his sternum.

"Well, yeah," he said. "I thought it would be really fun."

She made an indignant noise.

"What?"

"Well what about the band we were going to be in?" Joe, staring at the back of her hair, suddenly wished he could see her face.

"I kind of thought that . . . sort of fell by the wayside," Joe said. "I mean, we talked about that before we even got together."

"I really liked the idea. Now you don't want to? Is it because we're going out?"

"No. It's just—I don't know how realistic that idea was in the first place, you know? You were going to play guitar, I'd sing . . . and that was it, right?"

"Yeah . . . I dunno. We could probably find a drummer if we wanted to."

"Well, okay. You know, you didn't show any interest in this for more than a year, and now you suddenly want to now that I said I want to be in this other band."

Vanessa squirmed out of his arms to glare at him, arms crossed.

"Fine then. Just go be with Eva, that's what you want."

He felt a general warmth, as if it weren't hot enough already.

"That's ridiculous! I love you. I just thought it'd be cool to be in this band."

"Whatever." Her voice flattened. "Eva just wants you anyway."

"No she doesn't! Vanessa, you're really not being realistic here. This is a totally innocent, friendly thing. That's it."

"Fine."

Neither of them said anything. Joe wanted to, to make her see things for what they were, but couldn't think of what to say to get through to her. An uncomfortable minute passed.

The bell rang.

He called her that night. He had dialed Vanessa's number so many times that it was a familiar electronic melody. He could sing it if inclined: boop beep boop bap beep bap boop.

"Hey."

"Hi."

"I won't join the ska band if you don't want me to," he said.

She sighed. "I hate that you have to make it like this."

"I just said I won't join the band."

"If *I* don't want you to. You obviously want to do it."

"Yes."

"Well I don't want to hold you back from things you don't want to do!"

"Would it be that big a deal if I joined this band?" Silence on Vanessa's end. "Butterfly?"

"*Don't call me that!* Not now." To Joe's horror, Vanessa began to cry. There was something about the indistinct nature of sniffles heard over a phone. Joe only recognized them belatedly.

"Hey, hey. Shhh," he said. "It's okay. I'm not going to join the ska band. It's okay."

"I just don't want you to be taken away from me."

"I know, baby. I know. It's okay. I love you baby. I love you Butterfly."

"I love you too," she said, crying a little less. "I'm sorry. I just have a hard time sharing you, Joe. I love you and—I want you all to myself sometimes. I don't see enough of you as it is."

"I know. It's okay."

3

It was a full moon that night. Joe couldn't sleep. He'd made up with Vanessa, but the obligation to tell her about Spirit West Coast remained. They were leaving Thursday night, and coming back sometime Tuesday.

He gave up his phony stars and swung his legs over the side of the bed. He dressed and slunk through his house.

"Grrrrrr." The sound came from a corner of the living room, near the fireplace. A shape rose from the floor and ambled toward him. "Rrrrarrooo," Oreo said. She licked his leg.

Joe scratched her behind her ear. "You can come." He opened the door and slipped out behind her. This was different from walking to Vanessa's grandmother's in the middle of the night. He wasn't sneaking out. There was no rule against wandering where there was no city, no sidewalks or streetlights. Here were stars—diamonds unchoked by terrestrial light.

The full moon lit the earth so well he could've read by it. He walked across the lawn, Oreo bounding ahead of him with her tail flailing. They crossed the dusty dirt road and started down a path through the common grounds. Bats glided in the air. "I bid you good mosquito-hunting," he told them.

The sound of crickets was everywhere. He walked along the path, smelling the sweet and dusty scent of weeds and dead grass. He caught movement out of the corner of his eye and turned to catch an owl glide mutely by. He came at last to a small pond, filled with shouting frogs and buzzing insects. Moonlight flickered off the rippled surface and a solitary granite island jutted from its center. It was here that Joe fell to one knee. He thanked God.

4

He looked at the pond, at all the movement going on with bugs and things that liked to eat bugs. He wondered about the role of water in his life. Things always seemed to happen around bodies of water. With the rain cycle, the water he looked at then could be the same water he and Vanessa had kayaked over, had dipped their toes into and looked into lazily after making love. It could be the same water from the lake a year ago, that he saw the sunlight wavering through right before his head broke through the surface and his lungs released the air that was starting to burn. It was impossibly sunny, the water just short of being too cold as he looked around and took in the beach, the pine trees, all the people there for the youth group barbecue.

And her.

"You like to swim, huh?" she asked him, her own dry hair shimmering, gold shining from the hazelnut as he dripped back on dry land.

"Yeah," he grinned. He felt extremely aware that she was seeing him shirtless, and kept his gut sucked in. When they sat on a rock together to eat hot dogs, he'd put his shirt back on.

"Are we close to your house right now?" he asked.

"No," she said. "Meadow Lakes isn't nearly this far up."

They were together, not at school, not in tiny increments and not through smiley faces and text on an instant message screen. She sat next to him, in person and with her perfect leg even touching his own. He felt sure that other people noticed them, and marveled that he should be the one with the girl this time.

She seemed so at ease, in her element. She was a fantastic conversationalist; they could talk for hours and he'd never be bored. Funny, too. Meanwhile his own nervousness ate him alive. Was it only yesterday they'd flirted over Yahoo instant messaging? He was supposed to ask her out now, and she knew it was coming. But how to actually come out with it, say the words? She knew he'd never done it before—if only she'd ask him instead. He tried out phrases in his head, all the while doing his best to keep up his end of the conversation out loud ("Their new album is really good"). Would you like to be my girlfriend? Do you want to . . . go out? Everything sounded so awkward—why was relationship-talk so ridiculous?

He looked into her brown eyes (God she was adorable) and stretched his face into what he hoped was a charming smile.

"I like you a lot, Vanessa," he said.

"I like you a lot, too."

He opened and closed his mouth a couple times, moved his smile around and turned red.

She tilted her head forward, as though trying to hear something. "So?" she asked. She nudged him with a shoulder. "Do you have something to . . . ask me?"

"Doyouwanttogooutwithme," he mumbled.

"What?" she asked, teasing.

"Do you want to go out with me?"

"Yes," she said, and curled her fingers around his. She lifted his hand and kissed the back of it. Joe felt clearly the press of her lips against his skin, the first kiss she gave him. He seemed to feel it even afterwards, when he realized just how wonderful holding hands was. For weeks, he spent his free time remembering every detail of that afternoon, turning it over and smiling helplessly.

He couldn't say at which point like became love. He was infatuated with her from the beginning. He wanted to spend all his time with her and so did she. "Normally with guys I like to have space now and then," she said. "I never feel that way about you."

He kissed her for the first time on his bed one afternoon when they were listening to music. It was his first kiss, and he found that once he got over the terror of the thing and actually *did it*, it was pretty easy from there on out. Vanessa progressed from being a beautiful crush into someone he would happily die for. She told him she loved him, and when he said it back it was like saying the sky was blue. He had no doubt he loved her.

He longed for her painfully, and that she was his was overwhelmingly gratifying. And what unbelievable fortune that the most wonderful girl in the world would love *him* back! She could have anyone, he told her with earnest. Brad Pitt, Johnny Depp, anyone. "I don't think that's true," she said. "But you're the only one I want anyway."

Their friends were jealous. You and Joe have the perfect relationship, Vanessa's friends told her. "I told them it's because I have the perfect guy," she said to Joe. They wrote love notes to each other, poems, mix tapes and cds. They spent hours saying passionate things in the language of lovers, language which is spoiled like film in a darkroom when exposed to public light. But she told him he was her soul mate, her hero, her darling. She was his foreverlove, his angel, his everything.

And they said I love you, I love you, I love you.

Chapter 4

Joe's mom fixed a light dinner for two.

"Thanks, Mom." He put aside the comics page of the newspaper to join the rest of The Bee folded at the end of the table.

"You're welcome."

Joe bit into his sandwich, tasting the tuna, lettuce, and bits of celery and pepper between the slices of sourdough. "Mmmmgh," he said. Rosemary, his mom, also began to eat, but more delicately. The afternoon sun shone into the room through the blinds. After they finished, she would drive him to Tuesday night's youth group at the church.

"So," his mom said, "are you looking forward to our trip?"

"Um, yes and no." He chased a scrap of lettuce around his plate with his fork. "I mean, I hate to leave Vanessa alone,"—awkward now.

"Hm," she said. "You know, we're only going for five days."

"I know," Joe said.

"Is Vanessa a little insecure?" his mom asked. Her tone of voice wasn't nosy. It was the voice that he always knew he could confide in if he really wanted to.

"No," he said. *His* tone of voice made his answer into a puzzled quasi-question: *nnooo*—rising at the end. *What gave you that impression?*

"Okay." She shrugged. "I was just asking. A lot of girls do feel insecure in high school." She sipped her iced tea. "I think it's good that you're there for her . . . as long as, uh, she isn't needing you to be there for her too much. Does that make sense?"

Now he shrugged. "Yeah," he said, his tone light: *it makes sense, but it doesn't really apply, Mom.*

"Ask me about my day at school," she said then.

"How was your day at school, mom?"

"Really bad," she said, and laughed.

"Oh, Mom. I'm sorry. What happened?"

"Well, today was Read Around the World Day," Joe's mom began. She was a Library Media Teacher at Pine Ridge K through eight school. Read Around the World was a monthly event for the younger kids in which they read a children's book or two from a certain region in the world. To make it more fun, Joe's mom would also cook a few dishes from the same region. "And so I made that Thai curry, right?"

"Right."

"Well. I made a big deal of telling all the kids that the curry had peanuts in it. 'This has peanuts, kids,' I told them. 'If you are allergic to peanuts do not eat this BECAUSE it has peanuts in it.'"

"One of the kids was allergic to peanuts," Joe said.

"Sure enough, this girl comes up to me—'Miss Irviiiiiine, I'm allergic to peanuts and I don't feel good.' I'm like, *why* did you eat it then?—Only nicer than that, of course. And so then we had to take little Arianna to the nurse, and she threw up, and her parents had to come get her, and all in all it was just this whole big ordeal." Joe's mom—Miss or Missus Irvine to her students—daintily nabbed the scraps of chicken of the sea on her plate with her fork and knife.

"Was the girl okay?"

"Yes, she was fine."

"That's actually a pretty funny story," said Joe.

"Well it wasn't that funny while it was happening," his mom said. "Not when I'm worried about just *how* allergic to peanuts this girl is and just *how* furious her parents are going to be with me."

"Did you talk to the parents?"

"Yeah, they were fine. They were sane parents." Joe knew that there were plenty of less sane parents. Elementary school settings seemed to expose them—parents who thought their bratty kids could do no wrong, or parents who thought little leprechaun footprints made with flour on Saint Patrick's day were "too pagan" and probably even satanic. The yin/yang here was that elementary school staff and teachers were pretty much the nicest people in the world.

"Well that's good."

"Mm-hmm. You ready to go? Brushed your teeth? Got your Bible?"

"Yeah."

They left and drove along Auberry Road, the beautiful scenery of the foothills not making much of an impression on either of them because of the familiarity of it all. Yet Joe sometimes thought that they reacted to it more than others even so.

They passed an abandoned fire station, which was where Vanessa had given Joe his first blowjob (Joe felt squirmy driving by with his mom). Then they turned a curve and saw the church's sign, "AUBERRY COMMUNITY CHURCH" in white letters on the wooden sign. Joe's mom turned in and stopped the car on a painted "steal the bacon" court on the asphalt.

Teenagers milled about. Joe saw familiar faces talking in groups outside, leaning on the porch railing, and a few jumping on a well-used trampoline. There was Vanessa nearby, talking to a few other girls. He waved to her.

"Hi Vanessa," Joe's mom called.

"Hi!"

His mom asked Vanessa how summer school was treating her, and they laughed over some small joke before she backed out again to head home. Joe hugged Vanessa, rubbing her back between her shoulder blades.

"How's it going?"

"Good. I started a new painting after getting home from school."

"Oh cool—what is it?"

"It's this weird thing—pretty abstract. It's got people coming out of different doors at different angles, but the doors are in weird things like plants and stuff—I'm really happy with this scary Venus flytrap kind of plant. I gave it like, shark teeth. And then also the lighting is really weird. I've got it coming in at different angles and stuff."

"That sounds really cool! I can't wait to see it."

Vanessa's creativity had been one of the things Joe had been most attracted to in her from the very beginning. He marveled at her ability to draw things that actually looked like, well, real *things*. His own doodles still looked like endeavors the parent of a third-grader might stick on the fridge with a magnet declaiming, "Look what JOE did today!" The love poems she wrote him were in some ways better than the best sex they had. But still he loved the art she made for herself and no one else.

They approached the small youth building, and a booming voice rang out: "Jooe King! Jooe King!"

Joe laughed. "Hey Tom," he said. Tom strode forward with a fat man's swinging gait and reached out his hand.

"How's it going, buddy?" the youth pastor asked.

"Good, man," Joe said automatically. "How're you?"

"Can't complain," Tom said in his jocular voice. "C'mere, Vinnie." He gave Vanessa a one-armed hug. "Busy, but that's what I'm here for, right?"

The youth building was the kind of house you saw in halves being pulled down the freeway on big trucks. The two of them went in to join other high schoolers sitting on the saggy old couches that lined the walls. There were an abundance of posters up, saying things like "Put on the armor of the Lord"—with a diagram of a warrior, pointing out the shield of faith and the sword of the Spirit, among other things. Another said:

In the beginning there was
GOD.

There were snarky ones, too. One, simply printed from someone's computer on green paper said:

> "God is dead."—Nietzsche
> "Nietzsche is dead."—God.

That one always bothered Joe a little because it wasn't as though it proved any point—Nietzsche would still be dead even if he was right about God.

A pro-life newspaper clipping was also tacked up on the wall. It demonstrated how advanced developmentally the fetus is during the early stages of pregnancy and had an eye-catching quote from Madonna. Madonna, the clipping noted, was not pro-life, but said that she saw her baby on an ultrasound looking as though it were tap-dancing. "I could have sworn I heard it laughing." Pro-choicers were scarce in the Auberry/Tollhouse area; "feminist" a slur reserved for few—mostly teachers like Frau Lismore.

And between all the posters names were written in colored pencil. One day Tom had passed around the Crayola boxes and told everyone to write their name and the year they would graduate on the wall—Joe King, 2007. It gave one a nice sense of belonging.

When the lights went off Joe stood up next to Vanessa. She intertwined her fingers around his for the millionth time, and he smiled at it. A low humming filled the room as someone switched on an old projector and lyrics to praise songs appeared on an improvised backdrop. A few upperclassmen led worship, which meant that they stood at the front and played guitar and sang with everybody else. One of them was Joe's stepcousin (Tobias's nephew), a tall kid who would be a senior in the fall. He counted them off and then they sang:

> *Lord of all creation, of water, earth and sky*
> *The Heavens are your tabernacle*
> *Glory to the Lord on high*

> *Singin' God of wonders beyond our galaxy,*
> *You are holy, holy*
> *The universe declares your majesty*
> *You are holy, holy*

The room was mostly dark. Some of the kids held hands and swayed together in a line. Some people raised their hands, palms directed upward. Some nights Joe got that into worship, but that night he had too many things on his mind. As he sang he looked out of the corner of his eye at the way Vanessa's face looked in the dim yellow light.

> *Hallelujah—to the Lord of heaven and earth!*
> *Hallelujah—to the Lord of heaven and earth!*
> *Hallelujah—to the Lord of heaven and earth!*

They sang a couple more songs before the lights came back on and they sat again. The lovebirds' hands remained clasped together. The worship leaders quickly put their things away and sat down too, leaving Tom standing in the center of the room. He cleared his throat and began.

"How many of you ever feel stressed out?" His intonation made the question feel like the first part of a joke: how many of you ever feel *stressed out*? Tom continued: "The Bible tells us in Philippians chapter four, verse six, 'Be anxious for nothing, but in everything by prayer and supplication, with thanksgiving, let your requests be known to God.' What do you think about *that*? 'Be anxious for *nothing*!' God doesn't want us to worry about anything at all!

"Now you're probably thinking, well that sounds pretty good, Tom, but how exactly are we supposed to just stop worrying?"

Tom paced around the room as he spoke, the floorboards creaking underneath him. His white Nikes shone as he turned to face the different sides of the room.

"Well, it's actually beautifully easy, and it's all about completely trusting God. In Peter 5:7 the Bible says 'cast all your cares upon Him, for He cares for you.' So what you do is you take all your stress and all your worries about school and home and *life* and you say, 'Here, God. I'm giving all this to you, because I know that everything will be okay in the end. You said so. So I'm giving you the reigns. You're in the drivers seat, God, not me.' And once you do that, oh man, you'll feel so relieved. Believe me, I've been there. You will feel so at peace knowing that no matter what, everything's going to be okay, and you don't have to worry about anything, because you're just following the path God's set for you, and he'll take care of any obstacles that get in your way.

"Just *trust* God. He knows what he's doing," Tom smiled.

Joe felt his mood lifting. Tom was right. Here he was stressing out over his relationship with Vanessa, when of course everything would be alright with God on the throne. After all, hadn't God put the two of them together? They were meant for each other, were perfect for one another. He squeezed her hand, and she gave a subtle but utterly charming close-lipped smile. Without turning her head too much she looked into his eyes briefly, then to Tom again. They imagined that no one picked up on their little signs of affection, and half the time they were right.

He'd tell her about the trip, which was the day after tomorrow now. She would probably be upset, and he would have to calm her down, but in the end it really wouldn't matter. Years from now, when they were married, they wouldn't look back on this with any seriousness—if they did at all, it would be to laugh about it—"I can't believe how long you waited to tell me," 25-year-old Vanessa would say. "I can't believe how badly you overreacted," 25-year-old Joe would reply, and they'd just crack up over the whole thing.

2

They perched next to each other on a curb away from the others. Joe didn't have his arm around her as he would have liked to; this was discouraged at youth group. But they held hands, they never grew tired of holding hands, and before speaking, Joe raised Vanessa's hand to his lips and kissed it as she had done for him so long ago.

"Mmm," she said happily, and lay her head on his shoulder.

"Hey love," he said. "Do you remember me saying a while ago that my mom was thinking of us all going on a trip to the Spirit West Coast Festival?"

"Um, yeah."

"Well okay . . ." he sighed. "So I feel really bad about this, but she and Tobias planned the trip out a while ago and I never got around to telling you."

Her head lifted off his shoulder. "When are you—"

"We're leaving Thursday and coming back Tuesday."

"What? Thursday?"

"I know, it's soon."

"And you'll be gone for practically a week!"

"Well, only five days, my mom and Tobias wanted to spend a day or two in the area after the festival. But I'm really sorry I didn't tell you sooner."

She stared at him. Joe was alarmed to see tears in her eyes.

"I just seriously can't believe this! Everything was going so well, too."

"Everything's still going well."

"No it's not! Not with you going away for fucking *five days!*"

"Vane—"

"You're *always* leaving!"

"What? I am not!"

"Yes you are! You're always going to visit relatives in Florida, or at your dad's house where I can't even talk to you on the phone for a few minutes because of his stupid rules, or wanting to go to another country . . ."

"But I'm not going to Germany."

"Sure. You probably will next week. You're always leaving me behind."

"Vanessa . . ."

"Why don't you just fucking leave me behind forever. That's what you really want to do."

He touched her shoulder. "Vanessa, I love you."

"No you don't!"

"I, uh, y-yes, I do love you, Vanessa. Please don't cry." It startled him to realize he was close to crying himself.

"How can I not cry when I love you and you're always leaving me?"

"Look, Vanessa, it's not even like I'm choosing to go on this trip," Joe said. "My mom wants to go and I just kind of have no choice."

She kept crying, softly, and Joe tried to hold her. She pushed him away.

"Everything will be okay, darling," he said.

"No it won't"

"Yes it will—listen, remember how during youth group Tom was talking about how we actually never need to worry about anything? Because God takes care of everything for us. We only need to trust in Him. You know what I mean?"

"God hates me."

This blindsided him. "What?"

"God hates me," she said in a low voice. Her sobs had subsided into sniffles. "Why else would he let everything bad happen to me? He's punishing me for being a bad person."

Joe knew that in "everything bad" Vanessa was lumping everything together from her abusive grandparents who raised her to the current situation.

"No, baby, that's not the way God works," he said softly. "God loves you more than you can possibly imagine, that's why he died so he could be with you."

"When I pray," she said, "I don't even feel like God is listening. And I never feel like he's with me, or trying to show me something, or anything."

"It's hard sometimes. But you shouldn't get discouraged and push God away from you—He only wants to be close to you."

"Hm," she said.

"Baby," he said, not daring to call her Butterfly. "Do you want to pray together?"

"No, I don't."

"Are you sure?"

She stood up. Joe looked up into her face, pale against the twilight sky. He wanted to kiss her, thought it might comfort her, but knew he wouldn't dare, here at church. He stood up too.

She pointed to the parking lot. "My mom's been waiting."

"I'll call you."

"No. There's nothing to be said."

Still angry, then. But with a new, cold, calmness that was rare for her. He used to feel affection for her temper, and thought of her as his own little spitfire. That was when her outbursts were rare, troubles and arguments nonexistent.

"Okay. Goodnight, Vanessa. I love you."

"Don't say that right now!"

"But—why not, Vanessa?"

"It's not fair. You make me feel like a terrible person for not saying it back, but I *shouldn't* say it back if I don't feel like saying it."

Joe sighed.

"Goodnight."

He lay in bed that night wanting to be with Vanessa. Time fixed everything; if only he had all night to lay with her. It was hard, the increments for each other they had to fit in. But all he could do was feel sick to his stomach while she cried uncomforted in her own bed, miles away.

Chapter 5

"Od, please help Vanessa. Please let her know that you are there. Please let her feel your love, and comfort her. And let her know that I love her, too. We have felt your blessing on our love for each other, the life that we plan together. Thank you so much for that, Lord. Father, please give her that sense of calm assurance. I pray that you would prompt her to give in to you, to trust you, and that you will continue to watch over our relationship.

"Let this time of trial pass, if that is your will, God, and let us go on to love each other in a way that is pleasing to you, that includes you intimately, that we may devote our lives together to you, God, and bring glory to your name.

"In Jesus's name, amen."

Joe opened his eyes and lifted his head from the car window. He glanced at Peter Sandstrom, his best friend who had accompanied them on their trip. Peter was listening to his discman.

Joe replaced the cd in his own. He was excited about several of the bands they would see today, and listening to the music pumped him up even more.

The lyrics were fresh in his head when they arrived and Joe and Peter branched off to head for the rock stages. A screamo band was playing so they jumped in the mosh pit. Joe was there with the best of them, headbanging and shoving and screaming out the words when he knew them. Peter was propelled forward by the crowd, and pushed Joe with all that momentum. Joe went flying, exhilarated by the feeling of almost falling while bolstered by the fact that it would be hard to fall, pressed in by so many people. He was covered with sweat, his own and everyone else's, and to him it smelled like love, and community.

It was all about the music. It drove and sustained them all, and when the singer would let out a scream Joe felt a delicious mix of passion, aggression and joy made all the stronger by the crowd's amplification. It was about connection. Joe grinned and came at an emo kid. When he shoved him, he got shoved right back and stumbled backwards into a pulsing, swaying, jumping mass which held him up even as it pushed him further. Joe jumped as high as he could to the rhythm, careful to land on unoccupied spots of concrete. He beat his head, loving the feel of his hair whipping up and down. He'd gotten out of the middle, where the real action was, and dove back in.

When the set was finished, a Spirit West Coast official came onto the small stage and greeted them all.

"This is a place where we can all come together to find refuge in the Holy Spirit. I know you guys have all noticed this, but the world is a pretty dark place. It's a pretty Godless place. You can take it from me that God is real—"

Applause, cheering.

"—And that the Devil is real, too. And the world is the Devil's domain."

"So please, take advantage of this place, of this oasis of God's love within a desert where sin reigns. Have a great time and remember that we're all here to give praise and thanks to the Lord. We're all here to give comfort to one another. We are all warriors together in the fight against darkness and temptation, fighting to bring God's light to the world.

"But sometimes, the world can really get you down. Because while we're out the world fighting to be the light, to bring people to Jesus, Satan is throwing everything he's got at us. So if you're troubled, if you're wrestling with some tough stuff right now in your life, what I want you to do right now is just turn to a person near you and ask them to pray for you. Or, turn to the person next to you and ask them if they'd like you to pray for them. That's what we're gonna do right now, for five or ten minutes or however long it takes. Remember that God loves you, and that nothing makes Him happier than seeing all his children together like this, loving him back and loving each other, because we know we're all brothers and sisters here."

Joe turned to look at the people around him, feeling a touch of shyness, but feeling an inspiration stronger than that. He'd been moved by the man's words. Joe felt his gaze drawn to a brown-haired boy about his age nearby. He had a strong sensation of the Holy Spirit filling him, moving him.

"Would you like me to pray for you?" Joe asked him. The boy met Joe's eyes and nodded.

"Alright." Joe smiled. "What's your name, man?"

"Mike," he said.

Joe put his hand on Mike's shoulder and bowed his head, closing his eyes.

"Father, I pray for Mike," he said. "You love him so much, care so deeply for him. Please help him through whatever he's going through right now, Lord. Give him guidance, and strength. Show him the way you want him to go, God. But most of all, Lord, I pray that you would just wrap Mike in your arms, God, and let him feel your presence and your love. In Jesus's name I pray, Amen."

"Alright guys," the Spirit West Coast guy said when only a few people were still locked in prayers, some embracing as they spoke into the other's ear. Many had not prayed in the first place, or hadn't paired up to do so, but that was okay. "That was beautiful. When we help our brothers and sisters in Christ, we bring glory to the Lord. Earlier I mentioned how Satan is giving everything he's got to tearing us down, to tearing you down. Well, the reason he's doing that, my friends, is because he's scared of you. He's afraid of what you will accomplish with God in your heart. And he knows how it's all going to end, yes he does. He knows where he's going to end up because it is written in the Bible, and we know and the Devil knows very well that God's word is final. I'd like you all to pray with me for a minute . . ."

"That was a great thing you did, Joe," Peter said.

"I was happy to do it," Joe said. "I could just feel God very strongly, and there was no reason to deny it, you know?"

"Yeah."

"Oh, man," Joe said suddenly. They were passing by the booths, most of them selling merchandise or refreshment, but this one had a characteristic red and blue elephant on the side of it.

"It makes me so mad that they're here," Joe said. "They try to present themselves as the more Christian party, but they're everything that Christ stood against. They shouldn't be here, just lying to people who are here for God."

The sun beat down on them, and they moved on. People streamed by in all directions, going to stages or to large tents with more merchandise, or band signings. There were the kids, Joe saw more hardcore and emo kids than he'd ever seen, and the older crowd, the forty-somethings going to see Stephen Curtis Chapman or some other K-LOVE FM style Christian contemporary.

"Hey," said Peter, "when's the war gonna end, anyway?"

Joe's mind hadn't left the booth, either. "Not anytime soon, with the Republicans controlling everything."

"Did I tell you my brother saw his best friend get blown up in Iraq?"

"Holy shit!" Joe knew Peter's brother, who was a nice guy who liked to tell dirty jokes. "No, you didn't."

"Yeah." Peter's face grew dark under his glasses. "He said he never knew there was so much blood in a person."

They rocked out that night. You have to keep rocking out, even when your country is ruled by liars and murderers. Joe went home with a sore throat and high spirits.

Chapter 6

Vanessa was sorry. Joe was sorry. They made up. They had make-up sex when they could. Junior year was a bullet train that grew from a distant spot on the horizon to an unstoppable force with astonishing speed.

Joe's mood was unusually good for the first day of school. He had hopes that seeing Vanessa at least five days a week on a regular basis might heal their relationship. And he had a new determination this year to do well in school, motivated by visits to college campuses. This year, he told himself, 4.0. But what he was really looking forward to on the first day of school was the return to band.

It didn't disappoint. After his first period class, he hurried down to the music room, where a line had already formed outside of the door. First-day-of-school talk was exchanged among the band geeks—about summer memories shared and the filling-in of those not shared. Joe stood with his arm around Vanessa talking to their friends on the sidewalk beside the grass.

Finally the door swung dramatically open to loud, stirring music—and revealed a short, bearded grinning man. Mr. Greenberg was greeted with cheers. The students filed in, shaking his hand and then forming two lines. Someone tugged on Joe's hand and he took it. Joe looked across the room and saw familiar faces making their way around the room in a big circle, hand in hand, just as he was. The moment held, stretched out, and then they sat down on the floor.

Mr. Greenberg sat down on a maroon square conductor's stand and raised his hand in the air for quiet.

"Welcome back," he said. "I hope you all had a nice break—I'm very happy to see you again, and I'd especially like to welcome the new freshmen."

They clapped for the freshmen.

"I am Bob Greenberg," he continued. "I've been teaching music here at Sierra for eighteen years now. I'd like to introduce you to someone else as well—Toni, could you stand up?"

A slender girl with dark hair and olive-colored skin stood and smiled at the band.

"Toni is your drum major," Mr. Greenberg said. "Come to her if you need anything, and she'll help you out. If you don't already know her, you'll come to know her very well in the weeks to come, especially if you come to band camp—but okay, I'm getting ahead of myself."

Joe glanced at Vanessa sitting next to him. He squeezed her hand.

"Music," Mr. Greenberg continued, "is an amazing and a beautiful thing. It can affect us emotionally in the strongest way. It can make us happy, sad, angry . . . it can make us think of different things—memories, or places. What it all comes down to is that music has a unique ability to touch us. And we are here because we know that. We want to be the ones making people feel those feelings.

"We all have that in common. And that makes us a kind of family. Over the years we've worked out a formula for our family that works. Because, like all families, sometimes we don't get along perfect and sometimes we want to kill each other. "But—" he pointed to a white plastic sign above him. It was a painting of mountains with faces which sang and played instruments. Five lines of maroon writing underlined the painting.

"We can work out difficulties and even prevent them from occurring in the first place if we remember to CCARE." He pronounced it with a stutter: *kuh-care.*

"*Communicate*—when you have a problem with someone, talk to them about it. Tell them why you feel you do and try to do it without being hostile. This of course goes for me, too—if you have a problem with something I did or said, please don't hesitate to come to me and say, 'Mr. Greenberg, I need to talk to you about something you did that offended me.' I promise I won't be mad and I promise I'll listen.

"*Compromise*—be willing to meet others partway. This is very important, because two people come to the table with two different ideas of what a solution looks like. If both people are stubborn, and won't settle for anything less than their own ideal, neither person will get what they want. So work to find common ground.

"*Apologize*. Apologize when you hurt someone else's feelings. This is extremely important. You may be shy about approaching someone after an argument, but most people are willing to forgive and forget once you admit that you've done something wrong. Otherwise, hard feelings will remain long after the offense that started it all is over.

"*Recognize*. Everyone deserves your recognition as a peer and an equal. This also means recognizing people's differences. What this really comes down to is respecting others and others' ideas and opinions.

"*Empathize*. Try to see where other people are coming from. Keep in mind that they may be having a bad day, for example. That kind of thing."

Mr. Greenberg folded his hands. "And speaking of having a bad day, one of the most important things that you can do in this class is to remember that your attitude is a choice. If you're having a crummy day, do your best to leave it at the door. That will help keep the environment more healthy for everyone, and, more than likely, you'll feel better too."

He looked up at the clock. "We're out of time. Tomorrow we'll talk about band camp, which is *this weekend!* Have a good first day, everyone!"

2

Vanessa smiled as they walked out of the band room into the mid-morning sun.

"I'm so happy to be back at school," she said. "Summer school wasn't enough. I just can't stand being around mom and Rudy anymore.

"I know," Joe said, sympathizing warily. In spite of himself, he was beginning to wonder what things looked like from her parents' perspective. But Vanessa was in too happy a mood for thoughts like that.

As though reading this last thought, Vanessa stopped, put her hands on Joe's shoulders, and pulled him down for a kiss. He kissed her, but then had to fight to pull away.

"So public," he said, smiling sheepishly,

"Oh, just give me one good kiss," Vanessa said.

He did.

His new schedule was busy. He had three AP classes that left him no possibility to fit into Jazz band, so with a vow to take it next year, he joined Orchestra—just string instruments. Mr. Greenberg taught it; he taught all six music classes.

German 3 was the other class it was nice to come back to. Frau Lismore seemed to genuinely like every single student—no easy feat, or common one.

"Hallo, Roland!" she said to Joe, as he came in the door. "Hallo, Anika!" she said to Kay Robideau.

"Hallo, Frau," Joe said, and gave her a hug. In German 1, they'd chosen German names to use in class.

It was a typical first-day-back kind of class. Frau had them ask each other questions about their summers in German. What Joe'd done over the summer was forget a lot of German.

During lunch, in the bathroom, Joe saw an artistic endeavor he'd have to remember to mention to Hank and Eddie the next time he saw them. Writ on the wall was:

Here I sit upon the throne,

But it's Miss Peach I want to bone.

It seemed as good a toast to the new year as any.

Chapter 7

Thursday morning found Joe sleepy-eyed in the car, listening to the news with his father.

"Today in Iraq, A U.S. predator drone missed its target and blew up the home of an Iraqi family. It was a scene of chaos as the weeping mother of the family, the sole survivor, held the brains of her young child in her cupped hands as she screamed at American soldiers."

The translator's voice was calm over the woman's wails: "You come here and kill our babies. Get out, murderers! Why—" Joe's father switched off the radio.

Joe stared out the window. He made eye contact with a squirrel.

Ralph King said something.

"What?"

"I said war's a pretty terrible thing."

"Yeah."

"But sometimes it's necessary."

"Not this time."

Ralph snorted. "Hindsight is 20-20. It's easy to say now that the war wasn't necessary, but back then we weren't going to wait around for Saddam to bomb us."

Bullshit, Joe thought, and remembered Peter telling him they extended his brother's tour. "There was never any danger of Iraq attacking us," he said. "There was never any evidence, either."

"There was evidence, all right. And it didn't help that Saddam Hussein was so resistant with the weapons inspections, and the UN officers."

"The evidence was fake! From the beginning, Bush *lied* us into war!"

"That is liberal bullshit!" Joe's father yelled. "There's a big difference between faulty evidence and lies. After 9/11, it was a good thing Bush acted on the evidence he had, to make sure we weren't attacked again."

"Why bring 9/11 into this? Saddam Hussein had nothing to do with 9/11. That was another lie that Bush and Cheney used to go to war for oil! It was a flat-out lie that Saddam Hussein had ties to al-Qaida, and there was never any evidence at all for it."

It was a familiar argument and a tired one. Ralph countered every injustice Joe protested with unshakeable faith in power wielded righteously. It was the same fight they always had, and only the nouns were different.

2

Toni Emmanuel stood in the middle of a circle of band nerds. She was teaching them marching steps.

"That's about the space you'd need if you were to put your fist between your feet. Pull your shoulders back, and tilt your head back so that your chin is parallel to the ground. Put your arms straight down at your sides, with your hands closed and your thumbs pressed against your forefinger—as though you're handing someone an envelope, see? Everyone try it."

They imitated her.

"Good. Now there's also a verbal response to this command, so when you hear 'Atten-hut' you say 'Chiefs'—loud, get it?"

Later, after eating, they moved to the gym and circled up again.

Mr. Greenberg raised his hand and the students followed suit. The large space fell quiet.

"As a group," Mr. Greenberg said, "or as a family, we can be thought of as a chain." He held out his right hand, and Toni, sitting next to him, took it. "Please hold the hands of the people sitting next to you. A chain can be large, but if even one of the individual links in the chain is broken, the whole thing doesn't work.

"I'm going to squeeze the hand of either the person on my left or right. Then that person will squeeze the next person's hand. When your hand is squeezed, squeeze the person next to you's hand, and it'll go around in a circle and come back to me."

He squeezed Toni's hand. The squeeze orbited. Vanessa squeezed his and he squeezed his neighbor's, and there it went back to Mr. Greenberg.

"Good," said Mr. Greenberg. "Now we're going to do that again, but with everyone's eyes closed. I'm not going to say what side the pulse will come from. It could come from either side, or it could come from both. It is important that everyone is quiet."

Darkness. Silence, broken only by irregular rustling when someone shifted his position. Joe watched murky red waves swirl in back of his eyelids.

Finally Mr. Greenberg said: "Open your eyes." Sixty kids blinked at him under the sudden light. "That time it didn't work," he said. "Maybe someone didn't squeeze very hard or someone wasn't paying attention. But it's important for everyone to concentrate in order for this to work. We won't move on until we succeed. Please close your eyes again."

This time it wasn't long until Joe felt the guy next to him squeeze his hand, and passed it on to Vanessa. After a minute, Mr.

Greenberg had them open their eyes again. "Good," he said. "Let's try it one more time."

This time it came from both sides. Joe felt it first on his right side, then his left. Both made it back to Mr. Greenberg. Then they let go of each other's hands and moved on to a name-learning game.

3

Ten-thirty found Joe and Vanessa outside at a table. Joe looked at the stars, so visible in their multitude. He slipped an arm around Vanessa's slim waist. She sighed.

"You okay, Butterfly?" he asked her.

"I want to go home," she said.

"Why?"

"Mr. Greenberg doesn't like me."

"He likes you. Mr. Greenberg likes everybody."

"Not me—he thinks I'm not happy enough or enthusiastic enough or whatever."

Joe considered this. It was true that Vanessa tended to approach activities with a reluctant and—his mind couldn't find another word for it—sulky air. But really, Joe didn't think Mr. Greenberg even spent time thinking about things like that.

"I don't think he minds if you're not that enthusiastic," he said. "As long as you're not being really openly negative about things I don't think he minds."

"He wants everyone to be super-positive all the time, like you and Toni. He wants to go back to Disneyland again."

There were several layers to that statement, Joe thought. He remembered a couple arguments they'd had when Vanessa said he was too cheerful.

"Well," he said. "He want us all to be happy, because he likes us. But I think he realizes that we're all different people with different personalities too. He doesn't expect more mellow people to be giddy and laughing all the time."

"Hm," Vanessa said in an unconvinced way.

"Mr. Greenberg likes you."

She leaned against him. "As long as you like me I'll be happy," she said.

He grinned. "You know I do." He kissed her.

"I love you, Joe."

"I love you, too."

They looked up at the Milky Way. Joe could almost believe they might fall in.

4

Joe woke up gradually to the sound of others waking, their footsteps sending thudding vibrations through the gym floor. He rolled onto his back and thought about opening his eyes as he listened to the rustle of people unzipping sleeping bags and rustling through backpacks. In the music department, sleeping on gym floors was a part of life. He'd slept in several other schools' gyms on Sierra's tour in the spring. It had become a familiar feeling—one of restedness that you hadn't really expected from the hard floor. Overnight the sleeping bag had gone from being a little too stuffy to become the epitome of warmth and coziness. The hobo's womb. Joe opened his eyes and surveyed the gym. Girls slept on one half and guys on the other. He saw some padding out with towels in their arms, others sleepily pulling on shirts, and others still blissfully asleep, snoring lumps on the laminate wood.

Then, with a low buzzing, the overhead lights came on. "It's seven o' clock," Mr. Greenberg's voice said—Joe would have had to sit up to see him and he was taking things one step at a time. "You have one hour until rehearsal."

They played classics like "On Wisconsin!" and the "Notre Dame Victory March." There were also versions of "Are You Ready For This," "The Final Countdown," "Get Ready," among others. For Joe, it was always the same. In spite of his best intentions, he would never practice over the summer, and then feel it all come back as he played songs he had played a hundred times before, his out-of-shape lips growing tired and the corners of his mouth struggling to hold firm on the high notes.

They went out and lined up on the forty-yard line. Mr. Greenberg walked toward them with his floppy white hat on to protect him from the sun. Joe felt the back of his shirt already growing sticky as he stood between Jackson the soccer-playing Junior and Remy the gothic hot chick.

"What we're going to practice right now is just the glide step," began Mr. Greenberg. "Each step is supposed to be twenty-two and a half inches, so you should get to the next yardline in eight steps."

Glide stepping should look, he reminded them, as though you are moving forward on a treadmill.

"Band—atten-hut!"

"Chiefs!"

"Forward, march!" He clapped and chanted as they moved forward. "One and two and three and four and five and six and seven and line! Good!"

"Band—atten-hut!" Toni's voice was a drum-major's bellow from the gut.

"Forward, march!"

They moved forward in a one big line, sweeping the field. Joe wasn't the military type, but it felt badass anyway.

The people at one end of the line got to the end of the field before everyone else, and a chunk between the center and the opposite end got there a bit after. Practice made perfect—or as close to perfect as the Sierra High Used To Be Mini Band ever got. It had been almost twenty years since Sierra had competed at a field show tournament in the usual sense.

Most bands competed within their divisions for the highest rankings of music played and formations well-marched. They practiced all summer for the competitions—Visalia the second-to-last Saturday in October, Selma the week after that. Sierra, on the other hand, did practice, but at a little—no, a much more relaxed pace. They were listed in programs as an "exhibition band." Always the last band to perform, their field shows were twice as long as the others. There was the normal stuff-music and marching formations—usually at least one fairly complex too—but also dialogue, props, and a song and dance routine. They were a comedy show. The best thing about it was that the crowd—which was almost completely other bands and their families—genuinely loved Sierra. The jokes were campy, but to the crowd, who desperately needed entertainment after the stress of performing, and who were getting bored, Sierra was worth paying extra on the cable bill.

Mr. Greenberg never failed each year to tell the story of Steve Martin's stand-up beginnings. Martin never found success until he replaced his customary grungy outfits with a suit and a conservative haircut. The jokes were the same, cheesy and pun-laden, but seemed funnier because they came for the mouth of an anchorman. So Sierra still worked on marching. There was the glide-step, the half-cadence, the prance, diagonal marching, backwards marching, projecting to the audience, flanking, court turns—Sierra learned them all.

Every former member of a marching band will remember what a drilldown is. Determined not to go out early, Joe entered the block with the other juniors. Toni started them out with the easy stuff. "Atten-hut! Dress center dress! Left-hace!"

More than a few people groaned, having instinctively turned before Toni brought them back to attention. She was behind them now, and not being able to see her somehow made it all a little bit harder. Joe stood with his hands clasped before his chest, looking beyond the other kids to the end of the field and the red band room beyond that.

"Atten-hut!"

"Chiefs!" Joe bellowed with the others, bringing his hands back down to his sides as his head swiveled straight ahead.

She regrouped them when there were four left. Besides Joe, there was Thomas, Charlise and Ilse. Joe and Ilse went way back. They'd first become friends while acting out against their fourth grade teacher, a notorious grump. When told to "have a better attitude," they donned excessively large grins—maybe a little too excessive, because Mr. Ritter finally asked them why they were barring their teeth at him.

"Silent drill," Toni said. "Atten-hut!" Nobody said *chiefs*.

"Canceling silent drill. By the numbers. Right hace! One!"

"One!" they shouted, and pivoted.

"Two!"

"Two!" they echoed, bringing their feet together.

"Parade rest!" She waited. No one fucked up. "One!"

"One!"

"About hace!" Charlise fell for it.

"As you were, sir!"

"One!"

"As you were, sir!"

"As you were."

"Atten-hut about-hace about-hace. By the numbers." *She's going to be ruthless and finish us off now.* The spectators—freshman, sophomores, seniors and all the ousted juniors—were getting more excited now that it was just three people.

"Left-hace about-hace parade rest dress center dress attenhut parade rest attenhut parade rest attenhut left-hace left-hace right-hace left-hace." Now she took her time. "One . . . two . . . one . . . two . . . one . . . one . . ." Somewhere along the line Joe forgot the next command and turned the wrong direction. He grinned sheepishly, joining the spectators to scattered applause.

After that Toni marched Ilse and Thomas up and down the field, flanking them all around. In the end it was Ilse who choked and lost. Joe thought maybe that was better. Thomas was sort of immature and unpopular, and didn't win things often.

But then, the most innocuous things could set Vanessa off.

5

Joe came off the field and made a bee line for the water cooler off the side of the dusty track. He swallowed a dixie cup of water in one gulp, then filled the cup up again and sipped at it as he walked back to his girlfriend.

"Hey," he said—quietly, because talking was verboten. He hugged her from behind, feeling the swell of her breasts just above his forearms.

"Hey," she said—but her voice was upset again.

"What's the matter?" he asked.

Vanessa didn't always answer that question right away when she was asked it. But whenever she got around to telling what was bothering her, she told it with flatness and frankness, melodrama be damned.

"You're better than me at everything," she said.

Joe didn't feel concerned. He didn't even feel irritated. He just felt tired.

"Vanessa," he murmured. "That is not true."

"Yes, it is."

He sighed and looked out at the troops marching to and fro. "Look, let's talk about this when we're not around everybody and not supposed to be being quiet."

She sighed.

So they talked about it over hot dogs.

"Vanessa," Joe started again, feeling bolstered by the new food in his stomach. "You—" he thumbed relish into his mouth, then took a quick swig of Pepsi. "—are *way* cuter than me."

She didn't say anything.

"You are a more creative person—you do painting, poetry and drama on top of music—and not just band, you play guitar, too. You're funny, smart . . . did I say very cute?"

"Stop trying to be funny. God, I'm being serious here, and you act like it's just a big joke."

"I'm sorry, Vanessa. Why do you feel . . . like you do?"

"Because it's true! You are better at me than everything. Shit, I was one of the first people out today. It's just everything! I'm not smart, no matter how often you say I am, and everybody loves you and hates me—"

"Nobody hates you—"

"Yes they do! Everyone thinks that you're so great, but I don't even have any friends!"

"You do, too. There's Emily, and Kaitlyn and Peter, just for starts."

"Peter's only friends with me because he's your friend."

"That's not true. Just because he met you through me—"

"God, you always have to contradict everything I say!"

Joe stuttered. "Would you rather I agree with these negative and untrue things you're saying? 'You're right, you suck at everything and everyone hates you?'"

"Well, at least then you'd be *listening*!"

"What? I listen a *lot!*"

"No, you just argue."

Then Joe did feel anger. He picked up his paper plate and napkin and left. Vanessa, sitting on a concrete ring around an oak, began to cry.

6

Joe was thinking about how things used to be. Vanessa had apologized to him—a rare thing even back in the beginning of their relationship. "My back really hurts from sleeping on the floor," she said. "Sorry I'm a bitch." Joe thought it was more than that. "Come over after band camp," she'd added. "I'll make it up to you." But for the first time, Joe wasn't sure he *wanted* her to make it up to him. He tried to put it out of his mind—for now, anyway, he told himself—and just experience the rest of band camp.

Mr. Greenberg, as music directors tend to do, loved and believed in music. He believed that music was an integral part of life, second only in importance and beauty to love.

He'd grown up in Anaheim, and worked for years at Disneyland, where the park's fraternal ideals (likely different than the ideals which dominated in the Walt Disney Corporate boardroom) made an impression on him. Mr. Greenberg sought to lead a family of musicians. Graduates had a hard time explaining it to others. They were fearful of describing something that would sound silly or cult-like. From time to time Mr. Greenberg would remark that his philosophy really just came down to suggesting that people be nice to one another.

That night they piled sleeping bags at the foot of the stage in preparation for the trust fall. They stood on a chair on the edge of the stage, and fell backwards into the waiting arms of the other students, who passed each person back, never letting them touch the ground until the end. You didn't have to fall, and if you did, you didn't have to stand on the chair, but everyone had to be involved in the catching.

Joe was one of the first to go. In spite of nervousness, he decided to stand on the chair. Though he was facing the wrong direction, he could see the band in his minds' eye—wearing pajamas, looking up in anticipation, tightening their grips around one another's forearms. They shouted: "Three . . . two . . . one!"

He hesitated, then fell. For an instant the ancient voices in charge of keeping him alive long enough to reproduce panicked. They cursed him for a fool. Then relief surged as he fell into arms, dipped toward the ground but didn't touch it, and was passed back, faces grinning down on him. Long florescent lights passed haltingly above him.

He got to his feet and watched Vanessa, grimacing, fall; then Peter, who gave a Pillsbury Doughboy *woo-hoo* before he fell, apparently fearless. Then Kay and Hank. Last of all was Mr. Greenberg's turn.

He got up on the chair and crossed his arms in front of him. His band shirt was tucked into his Levis, a thin brown belt separating the blue from the maroon. He fell.

As soon as they caught him, the people in front hardly needed Toni's urgings. They passed him on and then ran to the end of the line. "Hey Mr. Greenberg," a student would always be saying. "Hello," he said. The line always disappeared behind his feet, and people raced outside the human hallway to reform it at the other end. They maneuvered him into the middle of the gym and toward the door. They bottlenecked at the doorway, then got him out. The sprinklers had just ceased, and the sidewalk and the lawn were wet and cool in a pleasant way on the students' bare feet (no shoes for the trust fall). They carried him into the night like some bizarre morphing caterpillar. They went around the gym, giggling and wisecracking about tossing him in the pool. Finally, they returned him back inside their small gym weekend home and lowered him to his feet under the bright florescent lights.

Chapter 8

The state of Joe and Vanessa's love was under siege. Fights were around every corner, exploding like IEDs. The heart's Anbar province spilled into the rest of the country. Religious fundamentalists held sexuality hostage. Sectarian violence probably already was civil war.

Joe made the decision to withdraw.

He was scared. Vanessa was prone to bouts of depression. She'd first cut herself in seventh grade, and had done it since, especially when she felt unloved. She'd told Joe that when she cut herself, she did it because she felt that she deserved to be punished. She'd told Joe, too, of suicidal urges. Yet once when he suggested she resume seeing a therapist, she'd become angry. "You think something's wrong with me?"

Of course getting dumped tended to depress people. She'd start cutting again. He knew her. What were the odds of something worse? He didn't know that.

But he knew things weren't getting better. That neither of them were happy. And he knew that if he ever had been able to lift Vanessa above the clouds of self-loathing all by himself, he wasn't able to any longer. He'd been with her for so long, known that he would always be with her. At the realization of pulling away, he knew he still loved her.

He had shuddered with impotent sadness at stories she told him—of her grandmother throwing her across the room into walls when she was a little girl. He'd imagined scenes she'd never described—her drawing that first red line across the smooth white skin of her wrist, watching the blood bead and feeling more abandoned than anyone on earth.

Joe kneeled on the floor by his bed—classic prayer posture, which he almost never bothered to take. He clasped his hands and lay his head between his forearms. He tried to release the tears lurking somewhere before their threshold.

"God," he prayed. "Father God please help Vanessa. Please watch over her. You know my heart and know that I love her so much. Please just let her come to you for comfort when she's hurt and upset. Please soften her heart so she'll come to you. And let her know you love her. Please God, take care of her."

It was a sunny day, with postcard perfect cotton balls dotting the sky. Music kids laughed and sprayed each other with hoses as they soaped up cars. The smell of water on pavement and suds running down a car's exterior imprinted itself on Joe's mind. *Remember me,* the smell told him. *Remember everything about this day.*

He wouldn't have chosen to do it at the car wash. But the maddening combination of no cars and very careful parents meant they saw each other most at school and youth group functions. So it had to wait until the end of the afternoon, when Vanessa's mother would come pick her up. Joe found that childish dependence more infuriating than ever as he waited to perform the task that would set him further into adulthood. Did popping a cherry make you a man, or breaking someone's heart?

They walked up the small hill behind the drugstore to talk, still in sight of the industrious fundraisers. Joe could guess what everyone thought they were up to.

He sat next to her on a granite rock, in the shade of an oak. "Vanessa," he said.

She stared at him. She knew what was coming. She looked beautiful, sad, vulnerable.

Joe said: "Things have been really rough for us for a long time and I think . . . I think it's time for us to . . . to break up." The words were out there, birthed into reality. "I'm sorry."

"I can't believe I trusted you," she said hollowly.

"Vanessa," he wanted to hold her, and hung back. "I'm really sorry. I know how much this hurts you, and it hurts me a lot too—" She snorted. "But I really think . . ." his voice turned shaky, and he sighed. "I really think this is what's best for both of us, you know? And what's fair for us—I mean neither of us have been really happy in this for . . . months. Obviously you're not happy."

"We used to be happy."

"I know, Butterfly."

She cried then, and he held her, silently giving comfort even as he severed the rope they had once tied around themselves, the one they'd secured with crafty fisherman's knots.

He kept expecting her to push him away, but she sobbed onto his shoulder, wetting his shirt so that he wore her tears he'd wrought until he changed an eternity later. She knew it was the last time he'd hold her.

At last she stood to go. "Don't be surprised if I do anything drastic."

In the end, she didn't. For a nightmarish while, Joe thought her suicide was all too possible. But though he would hear through mutual friends that Vanessa was cutting again, and knew it was because of him, she never stopped her heart beating blood for her to draw. Any contemplation of a suicide of his own was, for now, a fleeting indulgence.

He felt like a monster. He couldn't know that the failure of his first love was not unique, and that most relationships end in hurting or getting hurt. He fancied himself more of a man that day—it was his way of romanticizing pain—but he was too young to realize that for all its splendors, love is in this way a stupid thing.

PART 2

She upset Billy simply by being his mother. She made him feel embarrassed and ungrateful and weak because she had gone to so much trouble to give him life, and to keep that life going, and Billy didn't really like life at all.

-Kurt Vonnegut
Slaughterhouse-Five

Chapter 9

The band stood resplendent in their maroon outfits, polished white marching shoes, fluffed dickies and brave little bowties in a line stretching up to Toni, who wore black with silver buttons on her coat and a bowler hat perched on her head. Her chin was level. Her eyes were lasers. Beyond them lay a green field under a darkening sky. Selma High School's football field dwarfed Sierra's. In the course of their performance, the last vestiges of light in the sky would surrender to the October night, leaving the band lit by stadium lights. Toni brought her whistle to her mouth as an announcer's voice boomed around the area.

"And now folks, while the judges are tallying up the scores, prepare to be entertained by the Sierra High School Used To Be Mini Band! They come back every year not to compete but just to put on a good show for the audience, and we all love them so much! Under the direction of Bruce Greenberg; Drum Major Toni Emmanuel . . . Sierra!"

The crowd roared. The sound was enormous.

Tweee-eet! Tweet! Tweet! Tweet! Tweet!

Muffled *clop clop clop clops* as the band glide stepped after Toni, the portrait of solemnity, following her to the center of the field. The crowd had solidified from long cheers, whistles and applause to a single chant.

"*Si-er-ra! Si-er-ra!! Si-er-ra!! Si-er-ra!*" Finally, Toni stopped by her podium.

The band kept going. Still donning deadpan "serious band" expressions they kept going right off the field. They crossed the dirt, reached the audience-side bleachers, and climbed the steps. Parents of normal bands watched stiff-backed maroon bodies ascend past them. By then they were breaking up. Groups turned down aisles, avoiding people's feet and legs and crushing yellow popcorn kernels beneath their gleaming shoes. They infiltrated the stands, and then their eyes widened to reveal . . . confusion. Their jaws fell open.

"Have you seen the football field?" they asked audience members nearby.

The announcer's booming voice asked, "Sierra, are you ready?"

A trombone player standing next to a grandparent windmilled her arms. The grandparent was more used to things like baseball. "Hi, Mom!" the girl shrieked.

"Hi, Mom!" the band screamed.

"Ladies and Gentlemen!" Toni beamed. "Boys and girls! Cats and dogs, mollusks and protozoans, we HAVE—something very special for you tonight. We have for you a celebration of idiocy, an embrace of pig-headedness and a commemoration of cluelessness—ladies and gentlemen, the Sierra High School Used to Be Mini Band presents to you *A Tribute to Stupidity*!"

The crowd roared. From where he stood below the announcer's box, Joe saw Mr. Sandberry, a substitute teacher and world-class eccentric, filming them. He appeared to have ice cream stuck in his long beard.

"And as such," Toni cocked a shameless grin. "We're going to be playing some *really* stupid songs." She clicked her mic off and roared: "One, two, three, four!" She brought her hands up, a sorceress summoning otherworldly powers, then threw them down and wrought music. The band started up a beat recognizable to anyone who had attended an inane school dance, ever. When they got to the chorus, the audience, especially the band side, sang out without needing encouragement: "*Heey Macarena!" Baap!*

When they reached the final staccato and hopped to face the field, Toni looked up at them again. Comprehension dawned slowly. "But . . ." she trailed off, "you guys aren't supposed—come down here!"

The band climbed down to form a simple formation on the field. They played, and the audience knew the words, though probably none would admit liking the song.

"*It-was-an . . . itsy bitsy teeny weeny yellow polka dot bikini—that she wore for the first time today!*"

Sasha, their lone flag girl, frolicked with manic enthusiasm across the field. She wore a leotard covered with sparkling sequins and ran around kicking and waving her flags with no sign of pattern or plan. She did not have flags of different designs neatly and inconspicuously laid down at the front of the field that she'd switch out as the songs changed, that was the strategy of other, mere mortal flag girls. Sasha had a big rolling trash can at her disposal, filled with mismatched flags, banners, poles, hockey sticks and God knows what else.

The band separated in two, forming the alluring orbs and rounded triangle of a bikini. As the song wrapped up, the members who made up the bottom moved quickly and lo and behold there was a twenty-yard pair of hips wigglin' on the football field like it was a Shakira video.

Toni assumed a stern tone after the applause had subsided. "For the love of Sousa," she said. "it's about time we were a little more serious. Let's play something more *appropriate*."

"With—" she added quickly, "just a little bit of help from our World Famous Booster Parent Color Guard!" The devoted parents of band geeks stumbled out to make fools of themselves. It had been they who laboriously carted the sound system, the speakers, the red barbeque and porcelain toilet that adorned the field. One of them was dressed up as a gorilla. Another, a sad-faced clown with frizzy hair and flippers on his feet. Middle-aged, chubby and balding they came.

The heroic melody of the Indiana Jones theme trumpeted forth. The audience responded with joy—they were easy to please, really. All they wanted was a fun and familiar tune and some comic relief after too many hours watching marching bands in the sun.

The booster parents rolled out a gigantic rubber ball wrapped in duct tape—a DIY boulder. The band split down the middle as they rolled the boulder between them. They did it twice, and the second time one hapless musician was not so lucky. The boulder struck him as the band played the final measure of the she song. He spun and fell as if dying, throwing his trumpet high into the air, where it spun, the stadium lights glimmering visibly off the brass, before coming down to crumple and stick in the field. The kids, who had respect for instruments drilled into their heads ever since they were first handed one in fifth grade, loved this in a horrified, disbelieving way. They gasped audibly. They had no way of knowing that it was a worthless horn that hadn't played right in years.

It was time for the grand finale. Toni announced in a dismayed manner that she thought she was coming down with some sort of a fever—"the dreaded *disco fever*."

The "Hi Mom" trombone loudmouth framed her mouth with her hands. "SCATTER DRIIILL!" The band ran screaming like banshees in unorganized paths to their new positions. Some gathered around microphones in the front, most in pairs around the field. They hooked their fingers under the jacket fronts and ripped them off like Clark Kent in a phone booth.

Underneath were brightly colored frilly silk disco shirts. A lounge-style piano player got things started, and then a female soloists voice pierced the night.

"*At first I was afraid, I was petrified . . .*" Dancers revolved slowly with their partners. "*Thought I could never live without you by my side . . .*" the girl dancers placed their wrists to their foreheads, palms out, distraught. "*But then I spent so many nights just thinking how you done me wrong, and I grew strong . . . And I learned how to get along—and now you're back!*"

Joe raised his trumpet as one with the other brass and played. The rhythm section came in too, creating a liquid feel that made the dancers really move around. Other singers joined the soloist, making a breathy gospel sound. "*If I had known for just one second you'd be back to bother me!*" But now the brass broke away from the melody, soaring upward, and when the choir returned to a tune it was: "*We. Are. Family!*"

Ba da baa ba da da baa!

"*I got all my sisters and me!*"

Ba ba ba dah!

The dancers became jubilant, sticking to the clean and smooth choreography while clapping and spinning. Finally, with a last blast, they halted, pointing their fingers in the air while their other fist struck their hip.

They were borne out on waves of applause.

Chapter 10

Joe finished his German final and talked to a kid he knew as Heinrich. He was new to the school. He was from Clovis.

"What are you doing this weekend?" Heinrich asked.

"Oh, you know. Hanging out—I don't really have any plans."

"There's a party up at Shaver Friday night. You should come, it's gonna be crazy. Hella hot girls too."

"Maybe I will." Heinrich was being naive. Joe didn't hang out with any of the Shaver partiers. "Hey man, I was just thinking about this—how come you were disappointed that "Adolf" wasn't a choice for your German name?"

Heinrich grinned. He was a tall boy with brown hair, handsomeness marred by swaths of acne. "Adolf, Roland! After the great man!"

Joe searched his face for a trace of sarcasm. "Hitler?"

"Hitler was a great man. One individual who totally reshaped the world."

Joe looked to see if anyone else was hearing this. "What—you—are you one of those people who don't think the Holocaust happened?"

"No, I'm an admirer of the Holocaust."

Joe stared. Evil sat at a shitty high school desk two feet from him, wearing a Vans T-shirt.

"Are you joking?"

"No—look, you're a Christian, aren't you?"

"Yes, I am."

"Okay, and you believe in Heaven and Hell, right?"

"Yes . . ."

"And people who don't accept Jesus's gift end up going to Hell, right?"

"Well, yes."

"Okay. Jews, by definition, have not accepted Jesus into their heart. Every Jew that Hitler killed was going to Hell anyway. Hitler, who was a devout Christian, um . . . streamlined the process."

"Streamlining the . . . there are so many things wrong with that that I don't know where to start."

"What's wrong with it?"

"Well, as a Christian, I know that Jesus tells us to love one another, for one thing. Not kill each other. The Bible says to leave judgment to God—it's not our place to decide someone deserves to die."

Heinrich smirked. "That's your interpretation."

"No, it's the truth! God is a God of *love*, not *hate!*" Joe caught himself raising his voice. "I mean, as a Christian I can't believe you would distort Christianity to justify genocide!"

Heinrich shrugged. He seemed a little surprised at the force of Joe's objections. *What did he expect?* Joe would think later. *Is he used to being around Nazis?*

"Who's to say Hitler wasn't acting on God's orders?" Heinrich asked. "God's wiped out races before. You should read your Old Testament."

The bell rang.

2

"It was unbelievable," he told Peter at lunch. "I would never have thought that we would have Nazis here at Sierra—or neo-nazis, anyway."

"Yeah," Peter agreed. "That's uh . . . that's really screwed up." Alyssa, Peter's girlfriend, nodded. The three of them ate their lunches in the sun. Joe had encountered ugly anti-immigrant attitudes and even outright racism, but never . . . *I'm an admirer of the Holocaust.* His faith in humanity took a hit third period.

Vanessa walked past them without saying hi. Her new boyfriend's arm was around her waist. They started dating around the time Joe turned 17. It was the gift of jealousy—or not quite, because he didn't want her back. Call it the gift of embarrassing territorialness, like she was a tree he pissed on first. He went to the movies and Laser Quest with Peter for his birthday. It was just the two of them because he didn't know who else to invite.

Peter tickled Alyssa. "Stop it!" He did it again. "Stop it!" Joe checked his watch. He was beginning to feel the effect of his year in isolation with Vanessa. His friends had welcomed him back, but the fit was different. Peter and Alyssa's act went from cute to annoying real fast when you realized it was all they did. Hank, Eddie, and Kay each hung out in a different circle, with people Joe didn't know. So it was Peter and Alyssa, and also Ilse and a handful of other girls who only talked about the most inane things known to man.

He did see Kay in Algebra, reading what looked like the most enormous comic book ever made.

"Graphic novel," she corrected. "Here," she flipped through it. "What do you think of that?"

It was a drawing of a short fat woman having her shirt pulled up over her head by another young woman, revealing enormous flabby breasts.

"Pretty weird."

"Yeah. Well that girl's taking care of her retarded sister, so maybe it's mean to make fun of it. Anyway. You should read it! It's what got me through studying."

Joe looked at the cover: a young couple embracing in the snow. He didn't want to read anything about love after breaking up with his former soulmate.

"I haven't really been in the mood for anything romantic."

"You'll like it," Kay said stridently. Kay said most things stridently.

3

He read Kay's book the first night of Christmas vacation. The book was *Blankets* by Craig Thompson. He read it with eggnog.

When he finished it, everyone was asleep and the house quiet and dreamlike. The tears in his eyes stayed unreleased and burning. He'd forgotten how much power a story could hold—the power to reach inside of you, to possess your heart until you felt like a different person after you'd finished. Joe couldn't shake the feeling the book was about him.

Blankets was about a Christian teenager's first love. The sexy parts forced Joe to relive his own sessions with Vanessa—memories that he guarded against.

He'd never read a graphic novel before, but perhaps no other medium could have touched him this way. When he turned his eyes to see parted lips descending to breasts, barbed wire laced his blood. He knew the story's pain and it knew his. Joe felt his soul's void when Raina fell off the edge of the world, when Craig called to say goodbye even though he wasn't going anywhere.

Even flooded with memories, Joe didn't doubt that he had done the right thing. The book brought pain, but a good pain—therapeutic and cathartic.

Or mostly good. There was also an alien, haunting side to the book. Joe had observed with rueful recognition the hypocrisy and selfishness of the church and Christians in Thompson's story. But he hadn't expected the protagonist to lose his faith. One page of the book terrified Joe.

"My faith came crumbling down so easily." The picture showed a huge, humanoid black wolf with puckered lips blowing down the boards and windows of a little pig's house. For an instant, Joe felt absolute separation from God—one that would last into the afterlife. Craig's faith—both that of the character and the author, for the book was autobiographical—had been broken by questionable authenticity in the supposedly unchanging word of God that was the Bible. This was something Joe would look into, but not tonight. Tonight he would sleep, with a pain that signified slow recovery.

Chapter 11

"It's an awful lot of fuss to put up over one sweater," Joe's dad sneered.

Christmas happened all of a sudden. Joe spent the morning at his mom's house. She made a lavish breakfast for six people. Tobias's two sons, Jordan and Andrew were staying. They ate pastries, meat and cheese in the kitchen.

Joe pulled a long underwear shirt on above his pajamas and joined them. Carols played from their stereo. Jordan came in from the other side of the house, making Joe only the second to last one up by minutes. Their tree was glorious. There were myriad of ornaments collected over the years—a reindeer here, a wizard complete with orbed staff there, several Peanuts ornaments, and a few bearing legends like "Praise the LORD!" or "A SAVIOR is born!"

After a few hours had passed, Joe's mom looked at the clock and sighed. "I guess we'd better get you to your dad's," she said. Joe collected some things in a backpack, then said goodbye to everybody and got in the Subaru's passenger seat for hundred-millionth parental my-turn-now and the hundred-millionth Christmas. He would miss the larger Irvine party. Tobias' family were devoted Christians, which Joe appreciated, and they were warm to him, but he never really felt he fit in with them. Their Christmas parties might as well have been extended church services and their politics a right-wing minefield.

They arrived. Rosemary said Merry Christmas to Ralph and Jessica and left. The mood was different there. Joe had allowed Christmas to suck him into a maudlin mood, one that jarred painfully here. There was a tense silence that could mean his dad and Jessica had a fight earlier in the day.

Joe gave them each a hug. It was Christmas, after all. He and Ralph stiffly put their arms around each other. "I thought you'd be here earlier," Joe's dad said. "We're eating dinner with Jessica's family, so let's go open presents now." Joe went to sit on the cold leather couch. Ralph and Jessica King sat in chairs. From above the fireplace they never used, a Picasso reproduction stared down at them. She had twelve fingers and one breast half exposed, right down to the top half of her areola. Joe's dad passed out the presents, getting down on his hands and knees to retrieve them from the sparse tree.

Joe opened a card from his father before he opened the accompanying gift. *Merry Christmas to a son who has not fulfilled all my expectations.* Joe frowned, opened the card. *But has exceeded them.*

"Thanks, Dad."

He felt vaguely that he should be moved, but wasn't. The Hallmark print ran against every sentiment his father expressed to him in his constant criticism and commands. The card rang false in Joe's heart. Still, it was nice of him to pick out the card, to sign his name endorsing a kind sentiment, even if it was false.

As they took turns opening presents in a manner that felt suffocatingly formal, Joe stole glances at Ralph King. A gulf hung between them that did not obey the confines of the living room, spacious though it was. Joe knew that his father loved him, knew, even, that he loved his father. But it didn't make him easier to put up with. There was love there, a frustrated love that peeped through the brambles and thorns of their relationship wherever it could find a place. But there was hate there too. They were family, and they knew each other very well without understanding one another in the least. His mother told Joe once that Ralph's father was even more overbearing in his approach to child-rearing. From this Joe took sympathy for his father, but also a fatalistic fear that this pattern would repeat itself through him in the future, and that he would be powerless to stop it.

Joe's stepmom smiled and chatted as they opened their presents. She was a thin woman of medium height with short red hair. She also loved Ralph King in a complicated way. Their marriage was fraught with screaming matches, but she stayed with him, which mystified Joe. Her eyes looked tired above her little smile, and Joe suspected she felt the same way about the day's activities as he did.

An hour later Joe sat in his room reading a new book. His blinds were opened to let in more light, and the culdesac waited outside his window.

"Let's go let's go let's go!" Ralph King shouted, even though they were all ready. Joe went out to their green Toyota. It sat under the shade of a large willow. The dirt around the tree's trunk had been raked and scraped ruthlessly. Nothing alive poked from the surface. Likewise the grass on the lawn was mowed with regular devotion. Its short blades made Joe think of a new army recruit's high-and-tight. Most of the other front yards in this upper-class suburb looked about the same.

Mr. King's eyes widened when he saw Joe, and Joe felt an old and humiliating fear, as though he were still young enough to be spanked. *What did I do?*

"God damn it, Joe! Go put on a nicer sweater."

Joe looked down at the blue zip-up sweater he was wearing. "What's wrong with this one?"

"You look like a fucking slob, and we're going to have a nice dinner with Jessica's family."

"This sweater is fine!" Joe would have bet money that Jessica's niece and nephew would be wearing t-shirts.

"Go change your sweater," Joe's dad intoned in a low do-what-I-say voice. Joe was suddenly furious. He felt his throat closing up.

"I'm just going to wear this sweater," he said slowly. "It's. Fine. Please don't be a control freak."

"Joe, just go change your fucking sweater!" his dad shouted. "You are inconveniencing everyone by making us wait. Now go fucking do it."

Joe realized, not for the first time, that this was the same level of respect his father had afforded him his whole life. Whether he was five or seventeen years old, Ralph King expected him to jump with prompt and perfect obedience to his every command.

When Joe returned, having changed, his father raised his eyebrows. "It's an awful lot of fuss to put up over a sweater," he said.

Suddenly, in spite of his love for Christmas music, and even the Christmas spirit, Joe hated Christmas.

2

They drove to Tulare. They pretended to be happy. They drove back. There was a fight in the car. No one, father, son, stepmother—was spared. She cried. Joe did too, but hid it in the backseat. They got home. Ralph King made Joe take the trash out and they ended up arguing in the backyard. Ralph pushed Joe, and something snapped. He shoved his father back. Ralph King stumbled backwards, almost falling. *You hit me, I'll hit you back*, Joe heard someone screaming. It was him. *You want to fight I'll fight back*, shouted the Joe underneath himself. There was no fight. The night passed and the morning came and everything continued the way it was for a little while.

Chapter 12

Not many books feature the protagonist laying in bed a lot. It's not very exciting. Unless, of course, it's the sort of book where he is doing a much more than laying there and there is at least one other attractive person to participate in the more than laying. But this isn't that kind of book. Sorry if the first chapter made you think it would be.

So Joe was lying in his bed a couple of nights after Christmas, wide awake. Not very exciting to watch him there on his back, his hands behind his head and his eyes staring heavenwards, but there was a lot going on behind those eyes.

Ever since he had given his heart to Jesus at Hartland Christian camp the summer before sixth grade, Joe's identity had been defined more than anything else by the fact that he was a Christian. He threw himself into devotion. He prayed nightly, before every meal, and at any other time throughout the day that he felt like talking to God—to ask forgiveness for an impure thought or to ask God's favor for any reason—could be as simple as *please God let me catch the bus this morning*. He talked to his friends about Jesus, brought them to youth group. Both Peter and Vanessa credited him with bringing them to Christ. In seventh grade he had led Believers' Club at Foothill Middle School. He did all he could to love his neighbors, his enemies, to represent God's love.

And now that identity was in peril.

Blankets had opened a door in Casa de Joe and let in a torrent of doubt. Or was this the devil trying to get between him and God?

It wasn't the consistency of the Bible that concerned Joe anymore. He had resolved that to his own satisfaction. It was the concept of Hell, so central to Christianity that, for all these years, he had accepted unquestioningly. If Joe had explained Hell on his blog, it might have gone something like this:

*God is absolutely perfect and no evil can exist in his presence. In fact, nothing short of perfection could exist in God's presence.

*Since humans are decidedly imperfect, we need a way to repent and be washed clean of sin.

*The old school way of doing this was to slaughter an animal. Sounds primitive, but this was before Christ. Jews would sacrifice their most valuable livestock on an altar to God and thereby be freed of the incriminating filth of their sins, insuring their acceptance into heaven to be with God after death.

*Importantly, they would sacrifice animals regularly, as it is impossible for people not to sin regularly and be tarred all over again.

*But then God so loved the world that he surrendered his only begotten son so that whosoever believed in him would not perish but have everlasting life. Because of his immense love for humanity, God himself came to earth in the form of a man, and acted as the last sacrifice any man or woman would ever have to make.

*Upon this act, all anyone has to do to receive God's gift of eternal life is to believe in Jesus and worship him as God.

*If, however, an individual perishes without accepting God's gift, he or she will go instead to Hell, because they cannot be accepted into heaven with their sins still contaminating them.

*God desperately wants every person to enter his kingdom, and is heartbroken when they reject his gift and end up in Hell instead, where they are tortured and subjected to unimaginable pain for all eternity.

So the defense of the doctrine of Hell is essentially that God doesn't send unbelievers to Hell; they choose Hell by rejecting ample opportunity to accept God's perfect gift.

Why did that all suddenly sound like so much horseshit to Joe?

Is it really a choice if the options aren't clearly defined? The offer is not: here is a loving God, and eternal life in paradise, and there is Hell, a place of eternal torment. Rather it is, here is an (let's be honest, Joe thought) outlandish and supernatural concept. Devote your life to it and you will experience eternal life in paradise. Otherwise you will burn in a lake of fire for ever and ever. No one could *choose* Hell in a way that would hold up in a court of law. No, God sent those people to Hell, sure as shit. Joe couldn't see how they deserved it. *We all deserve it*, the story goes, but that didn't make much sense to Joe anymore either.

Did he deserve Hell? He didn't think so, not eternal torment, no matter what Tom, his youth pastor, said. Did everyone else? If Joe would permit any Muslim, Buddhist or atheist who lived a kind and moral life into heaven, how couldn't a God credited with infinite mercy? And if torturing non-Christians was wrong in this life, what made it acceptable in the next one—for eternity? Had Heinrich der neo-Nazi been right after all? Or at least logical?

And it was more personal than just "non-Christians," anyway. He felt a surge of embarrassment recalling a call to arms he had often made after being "saved."

"You may be shy or embarrassed about talking to your friends and family about God," he'd said, years before he was shaving more than his peach fuzz mustache. "But wouldn't you do that to save your friend's life? And this is even more important—it's urgent because if your friend dies without having accepted the gift of God's love, they'll go to Hell, and exist in agonizing pain for the rest of eternity." All the while fearing for his own father's fate, a lapsed

Catholic. Joe found himself wondering if the average adult pastor had really followed the Hell doctrine to its practical conclusion as much as he had at age thirteen.

It was absurd, Joe decided, to believe in and worship a loving God who would condemn. And so he wouldn't. There had been a terrible misunderstanding of the God Joe loved. God wouldn't do such a thing.

For a glorious, short moment, this appeared to be the answer. Joe achieved enlightenment. The Bible itself didn't go into much detail about Hell and the afterlife—that owed as much to Church dogma and Dante Alighieri as anything else. Joe could continue to live his life for God, but for God as he really was, a God of love.

Joe took a deep breath and smiled. But his mind, it seemed, wasn't ready to stop its train of thought—only to switch tracks.

He thought of nights past when all he could think about as he lay in bed were slinky female forms: the feel of a girl's pelvic bone beneath bare skin, supple breasts with pert nipples. His dick would be a sentinel, hard and upright straining against the sheets. Joe would try to think of other things, to drift off because to entertain lustful thoughts was wrong and to masturbate was a sin. But hours—hours!—would tick by with his brain buzzing and his cock yearning, until with an inner groan he would give in.

When he came the drizzle on his belly was accompanied by a sick feeling of shame and disgust with himself. The next morning he would pray for forgiveness again as he showered, trying to wash the sin off his body along with the dried semen and remember the last time he promised it would be the last time, and the time before that. He would pound his fists against the walls of the shower and breathe in the steam and the shame would work itself deeper into his heart's core.

Joe thought of this and asked himself: *if there's no Hell to fear, do I really want to live my life under this regime of rules? Do I really want to continue "being Christ to the world?"*

Christianity had never been a religion of love after all—it was a religion of fear through and through, and the moment he realized that was the moment he left his faith and never looked back.

Joe had a moment of heart-in-throat vertigo, where he stepped into the void he had seen Craig Thompson fall into, and looked around with his eyes wide and his arms held out for balance. His identity, his life and worldview for the past ten years or so pushed away, discarded. He had always accepted it as selfish, small-minded and shortsighted to live for oneself, but—perhaps it could be beautiful.

Chapter 13

The return to school. That sun around which a teenager's life makes its orbit. It was bitterly cold on the January morning the Chieftains came back from Christmas break. The air was dry and students huddled, bodies buried under layers of cotton, flannel, denim, jackets, scarves, hats. The Californians yearned for the return of warmth. The mountains ringing the school were powdered with white under the gray sky.

Perhaps enlightenment is not all happiness. Joe was one of few who could cast off the superstitions of his upbringing. He couldn't help but think of the years he had wasted. Perhaps one of the most powerful forms of anger is born of the realization that one has been utterly hoodwinked. The only comfort he could draw was that those who had bamboozled him had been just as deceived themselves—tricked by centuries of dogma. But to think of all his maddening efforts toward purity, and of how many times he'd stepped on a soapbox to expound the wonders and calling of God the father, the son, and the holy ghost . . .

But now he was free. When Joe went to Biology later that day, it was science as he had never known it before. The sun seemed to come out specifically to gleam off the silver faucets on the lab desks as Mr. Mozello, today donning a white lab coat with a bison glaring from its back, began his powerpoint.

Natural selection. As though it had been scheduled specially for Joe's flight from religion. Joe hungrily followed the bird's beaks from a place called Galapagos. No more doublethink! Heritage and natural selection were obvious. Evolution was intuitive, undeniable to logical thought. And he no longer had to disbelieve it—to reserve judgment, harbor doubt out of faith. We find it obvious that Helios never really flew a fiery chariot around the earth, but how humankind still clings to its other tribal explanations—and how many years after Darwin?

Art still exists without God, Joe found in Orchestra—perhaps better than ever. The pads of Joe's fingers pressed against the humming strings of his violin while his right arm worked the bow. Wasn't there something beautiful in all of this? Human beings, out of nothing more than their imaginations, had crafted patterns, ideas, and stories to arrest the soul and make the audience weep with joy and sorrow. Human ingenuity had discovered beauty in the different pitches of sound, in the patterns of percussions. It had bound taut strings of different lengths to a resonant object, and then fastened a stick with stretched horse hair so that anyone could recreate what another human being had written; so that anyone had almost limitless potential to create anything from the instrument.

In Christianity, the human race and the individual were nothing. Praise songs were sung and sermons paced to in youth group mobile homes and in polished megachurches on the insignificance of me and I and you and us and we compared to GOD. God I am lowly, God I am sinful, worthless, disgusting, but You . . . *You* are everything.

No longer.

Joe was loosening his bow to put back in its case when Mr. Greenberg touched his shoulder.

"You played very nicely today, Joe. Have you been practicing?"

"Not as much as I should be."

"Well, you're improving very quickly." This was Joe's first year playing violin. He left glowing from Mr. Greenberg's praise.

As he went on his way he spotted Kay, walking by herself. Impulsively, he ran to her back and threw his arms around her.

"You changed my life!" he exclaimed.

"Aaah!" she screamed.

They laughed. The blue swimming pool sat still beside them behind a fence, as if it knew it had no business existing in winter.

"I changed your life?"

Joe felt a little embarrassed now by his enthusiasm. He realized that he had no idea where to begin, how to vocalize the personal paradigm shift that had occurred within him over the break.

"Well, I read your—oh, yeah!" He retrieved the thick book and handed it to Kay.

"Oh yeah," she said. "I forgot you had this."

"Well, I finished it," Joe said. "And . . . it really affected me."

He told her the rest as they mulled toward the quad. A longtime atheist, she congratulated him. It was surreal how similar it was to Christians' congratulations when someone had just been brought to the Lord.

The two crossed the quad, past the tent where the jocks and preps hung out and toward one of the yellow tables. Joe realized that he was following Kay to one of the tables at the edge of the quad near the classrooms, where her friends were hanging around, talking and laughing.

Joe wasn't very shy, but he was shy enough. It's the kind of thing that sticks around and evolves years after the age when one could hide from strangers behind a mother's knees. It becomes a fear of embarrassing yourself in front of the very people you'd most like to know and be best friends with. When Joe's mom had married

Tobias, Joe had been relieved that he wouldn't have to switch to a different elementary school—it had been unthinkable.

"No, no," a boy said. "There can never be another Joker as good as Jack Nicholson."

"I was like, are you serious?" a girl said at the same time to her friend. "You think lying to my friends is going to impress me? And—"

"The thing with Mr. Krakauer is that when he's nice, he's great. But—"

Joe needn't have worried. Everyone was talking at the same time and didn't even seem to notice him.

"Hi Joe," Eva hugged him. "Long time no see."

"Yeah," Joe said, and started to say more—about the music they both liked, maybe, or some anecdote from summer school, but then with an apologetic glance, Eva returned to the conversation she had been having.

Joe shadowed Kay and felt relieved when the bell rang.

2

Rosemary Irvine pushed her hair out of her eyes and aimed the hose toward a fern in the center of the garden. Some of her plants could survive the winter but none but the cactuses could survive drought. The spray arced through the air, drops catching the sunlight and making a rainbow in the mist.

She saw Joe.

"Hey sweetie. What's up?"

"Oh, nothing much. I just wanted to let you know that you don't need to drive me to youth group today."

He was nervous. She didn't know where this was going yet.

"Lots of homework tonight?"

Joe took a breath. He'd planned how he would say his half-truth, and he'd picked a time when Tobias wasn't around. "No," he said, "I've decided to . . . take a break from Christianity for a while."

She didn't respond right away. She held the water shower over the fern for a few long seconds more, then clicked the button on the underside of the handle and shut it off. She looked at Joe with an expression that said she was only trying to understand. He could feel himself starting to break under that look, and he steeled himself against it.

"Taking a break from Christianity?"

"Yeah."

Now her face showed concern: "Why?"

Joe tried to keep his voice neutral. Without effort, this would turn into a plea, or apology.

"Well, I feel like it's a lot of pressure, personally, for a person to always be trying to be Christ to the world, to be trying to interpret and understand God's path and plan for them . . . so for a while I'd just like to try . . . living for myself." He couldn't stop his voice from rising on this last phrase. He was vocalizing all that was seen by the Church as selfish and sinful.

"You've felt like you're under pressure?"

"Yeah."

"Hm." She nodded slowly. "It's not . . . supposed to feel that way. I mean, there's a lot of temptation . . . but you've always been a good kid."

Joe smiled weakly.

"Have you prayed about this?"

"Yes." It was true.

"Do you . . . still believe in God?"

"Yes." In truth, Joe was undecided. Each day he believed in God less. But for now it was enough for him to know he didn't want to worship God as he'd known him.

She nodded again. "Okay. And you don't want to go to youth group anymore."

He nodded.

"Tom will miss you."

Joe shrugged.

"Okay," she said again. She went parental. Her eyebrows raised above her face, still youthful looking in spite of faint age lines around her eyes and mouth. Joe knew from pictures that she'd always looked younger than she was. She'd turned fifty that fall.

"I still," she said, speaking slowly, as if to communicate the immovability of her words, "would like you to come to church with us when you're not at your dad's on Sundays."

"Okay."

"Okay. I love you, sweetie." She hugged him. It made him feel like crying. "God loves you too."

3

Winter dragged on. Joe felt increasingly troubled. He found himself checking his watch during break and lunch, and all too often time seemed to be moving even slower than during class.

He had a sneaking suspicion that his friends were shallow and inane. He would always love Peter—he had been there for him during his parents' divorce and all the skirmishes in Joe's long, never-ending conflict with his dad. He'd even stayed in touch with him when Joe so self-centeredly cut himself off from everyone who wasn't Vanessa Grey. But even if he felt guilty for it, he couldn't deny that Peter was no paragon of maturity in the eleventh grade.

His other friends weren't much better. Ilse and her girlfriends spoke disparagingly of THE PREPS, but might in the same breath introduce a discussion on shopping worthy of half an hour's earnest discourse. Joe would try to introduce topics, but more often than not these forays were protested—politics was a dangerous thing to talk about—far too prone to disagreement and hurt feelings, they said.

He tried to expand his social environment. One day he just followed Hank after they got their food in the cafeteria. Joe kept talking, never hesitating where he'd usually branch off to his own clique. They joined Hank's friends on a knoll near the math wing.

Most of them were seniors. They were smart and irreverent, and their conversation was peppered with pop culture and political references. They were the kind of people Joe admired, which made him petrified of making a fool of himself.

He sat on the grass and tried to look like he belonged there. Nobody paid him the slightest attention. A few times he made eye contact with someone, then hastily broke it off. Waiting for the bell to ring was purgatory. Later, he kept picturing himself as they must have seen him, sitting quietly at the perimeter, trying to sneak into popularity.

He only looked forward to going home to read. He could always find friends in a book.

Chapter 14

Joe knew it was coming because it always happened the same way. He waited for it in much the same way he waited for the footsteps to reach his end of the hall, carrying his father with all his disappointment.

A quick rap on the door, and Ralph King was in the room. Joe's progress report was in his hand.

"Did you finish your homework?" He sat down.

"Yeah," Joe said. He sat on his bed, a book folded face down next to him.

Ralph King nodded. "So," he began slowly, "do you have anything to say about your latest grades?" Joe's dad was often unpredictable, and this was a slightly new tack. Joe knew it would lead to the same place. Mr. King played nonchalant, leaning back in the chair with his arms on the armrests, his head cocked slightly as though to say: *go on*.

Joe shook his head. "No . . ."

"Well," Ralph King said, looking down at the grades the school had mailed him and raising his eyebrows, "they're . . . crap."

Joe didn't say anything.

"You're doing well in English, good in History . . . then you've got As in your music classes, so that's important for your GPA but doesn't really . . . matter otherwise . . . and then you've got a B in

Biology and a C in Algebra." He looked up at him, eyebrows still raised. Joe shrugged.

Ralph King glanced down again and shook his head, his mouth set firm. "This . . . is not good. You shouldn't be getting Bs and certainly not Cs in any subject."

"The rest are As," Joe said. "And that B is in an AP class."

"Just because it's an AP class doesn't mean you can slack off and get mediocre grades. Bs are mediocre. Cs are . . ." he shook his head again, "unacceptable."

Joe said nothing. He didn't see the point.

"You're a smart kid," his dad said. "You're lazy. There's no reason you shouldn't be getting straight As, including in Algebra."

He was lucky to ever get a compliment from his father that wasn't buried in a reprimand.

"So, until you bring them up, you will be spending all weekend, every weekend doing yardwork for me."

"What?"

"There's plenty of stuff that needs to be done. There's always raking and mowing and dog shit duties. Then my fence is starting to fall apart and the hedges need trimming . . . for that matter the whole house could use a new coat of paint. Once you get your act together, this won't even be an issue."

Joe just shook his head disgustedly. But the desire to argue dissipated. His protest wouldn't change his dad's mind. Years ago, his mother had talked him out of challenging his dad's share of the joint custody, though he couldn't remember ever not coveting the idea of breaking from his dad. He knew he was powerless.

"It's not like I want to be a jerk, Joe," Ralph King said. "You start making an effort, and I'll be happy to let you do whatever on your weekends. Until then," he shrugged, "lots of work needs to be done here."

"Whatever," Joe mumbled. His dad smirked, allowing him the impotent last word. And that was all.

2

Spring came at last, and the foothills were at their most beautiful. Joe watched green hills roll by through the school bus window. Flowers peeked out of meadows and streams full of melted snow from the mountains glimmered as they wound and twisted like snakes in their shallow canyons.

The music kids had new material to learn. They would tour in May. They'd play three SoCal high schools before bailing to Disneyland and Universal Studios. Their new music was the *Pirates of the Caribbean* score. It was absurdly fun to play.

After they played it clumsily through for the first time, Mr. Weinberger set aside his conductor's stand to give the announcements.

"All sections will be held this week," he said. "Percussion today, brass tomorrow, and woodwinds Wednesday. Next Friday is our parent information meeting for any parents with questions or who just want some more information about tour—that's absolutely necessary for any parents interested in chaperoning . . .

"Drum major tryouts!"

Joe listened closely.

"If you're interested in doing what Toni did and is doing so well this year, practices for drum major tryouts will start next week. The drum major of course has a major role in our field show, as well as helping me a lot and being a leader during the whole year—anyone is welcome to try out—again, that's a week from today that practice starts, not tryouts, okay?" He waited for questions, then looked up at the clock. "Let's take it from *The Black Pearl* again."

Joe stared through Mrs. Waters and the blue and red figures and equations she wrote on the dry erase board. He wasn't following the lesson, and wasn't trying to. This was math, where his C was *unacceptable*. His father would never understand that his threats didn't make Joe want to try harder. He polluted what pure desire Joe had to learn, replacing it with self-defense. In this frame better grades meant victory for Ralph King and defeat for Joe. There was no good direction to go, and so he stayed still. He was going numb.

He turned over his hatred for his father in his mind. Joe's mother, as far as Joe had analyzed it, seemed to feel that if she raised Joe with morals of kindness and sincerity, and loved him, he ought to grow up okay. Joe's dad had raised him to be obedient to Ralph King. He found that he couldn't remember ever not having mixed feelings about his dad. One of his earliest memories was of crying while his father teased him, saying that Joe would have to toughen up to make it in school.

And Joe didn't have a lot of good friends—whose fault was that? Mostly his. But he thought it could be factored in that he was never available on the weekend in the foothills—he'd be in Fresno at his dad's, most always. Probably weeding or raking, too, so was his dad's threat even much of a change? And Joe knew that he felt more comfortable around girls than guys, found it easier to make friends with girls and easier to make small talk with Eva than Eddie. Couldn't that be traced back to his asshole father figure?

But anger is a temporary emotion. Like a flame, if it's contained rather than unleashed, it will sear before smoldering into sadness, leaving glowing embers every bit as dangerous as fire. Joe lay on his bed of coals like an old-time fakir. He burned slowly.

3

Rosemary Irvine had a long day. But before turning in to bed with a cup of chamomile and her nightly devotional, she knocked on her son's door.

"Come in."

She leaned framed in his doorway. She wore the earrings Joe gave her for Christmas.

"Night Sweetie. You should probably go to bed soon."

"Okay."

"Whatcha reading?"

Joe held the book up so she could see the cover. "*Mostly Harmless*," by Douglas Adams.

"Is it funny?"

"Yeah," Joe said, though the novel was more gloomy than any of the other *Hitchhiker* books.

"Hm," she said. "Is he still writing?"

"No, he died just a few years ago of a heart attack. He was only forty—or fifty, I can't remember. Too young to die."

"Bummer."

"Yeah. I hadn't heard of him until after he died." He motioned toward the Martin Luther King poster he had on his wall. *Darkness cannot drive out darkness*, the quote on it read, *only light can do that. Hate cannot drive out hate; only love can do that.*

"MLK died years before I was born," Joe said. "Douglas Adams is dead. John Lennon. One day Stephen King and Al Gore will die and all my heroes will be dead."

One day you'll die, he thought but did not say.

She came in and sat on the bed. "Well, yeah," she said. "That's kind of one of those facts of life, yaknow?"

He laughed in spite of himself.

"Joe, what you have to remember is that these great people who are your heroes . . . there are a lot of people out there just like them—who maybe didn't get published or decided not to go into politics. There are a lot of really good people out there with really good ideas."

She looked through his wall, the way people will when they think about the past. "I used to want to be famous, you know. I used to want to be president. I thought that it could be *so* simple.

I would just get in there, and convince everyone to just . . . think like I did—make the world a better place. Now I wouldn't go into politics for anything.

"But I could've been famous. I could've. I could have been a great country singer." Joe saw she meant it and believed her. "Just not the direction life took," she said. "And that's okay."

Later he would think that Mr. Greenberg was one of life's great heroes that nobody knew about. He went to sleep thinking of the alternate universe out there where his mother was Willie Nelson's protégé. Vanessa was less insecure and just a little more intelligent. She and Joe were still together and in love.

Chapter 15

Toni sat forward on the conductor's podium. The big room held only her and four others: Ilse, Hank, Joe, and Thomas, who'd won the drilldown in the fall. Beyond the piano they could see Mr. Greenberg typing in his office.

"Okay," Toni said. "So, first I just want to tell you guys what being a drum major is all about. The most important part of the job," she thumbed behind her, "is just helping Mr. Greenberg with everything, big and small"

The drum major hopefuls nodded.

"He won't just ask your opinion on things to be nice. He trusts and relies on his drum majors. The other role for the drum major is to be there for the students. Just like Mr. Greenberg, you have to always seem happy because that's part of what makes the music department a special place. You have authority when you need it, but you guys know that ordering people around is not really how we do things. You have to get to know everyone, be friendly and approachable. Just like with Greenberg, people will be serious about learning music and behave accordingly at concerts and on tour and everything because they have respect for you, and don't want to let you down. We lead by example, and that means above all, having the right attitude all the time. It also means not being a big partier—not being known for involvement with drugs or alcohol. You have to be able to handle that."

Joe thought he'd be okay on that front.

"Everything else . . ." she shrugged. "—Is just technical." She smiled. "But I don't want to lecture you guys. I know you're here because you love the music department.

"The audition itself consists of three parts." She counted on her fingers. "There's conducting, where you conduct along with a recording of the Star-Spangled Banner, and a little parade segment just outside on the pavement. We'll practice both of these today, and the third part is an interview that everyone does privately with me and Mr. Greenberg. Any questions?"

Joe had one. "What kind of questions should we expect at the interview?"

"Well," Toni smiled again. "We're actually going to keep those to ourselves until the interview." Which was the answer Joe had expected.

She stood up. "We'll start with conducting. When you're conducting," she demonstrated, "you'll be standing up straight, with your shoulders back and your chin up, and your hands, at least to start with, held out at about the height of your face."

They mimicked her.

"Your palms are out and your fingers," she said, noting a few unpracticed hands, "are together. That's important because when you're conducting across a football field, your hands become so small that the band needs to see them as solid objects.

"Four/four time is the most common signature by far. That's down," she arced her hands up above her head before bringing them down together to chest level. "In . . ." they came in together. "Out . . . up." She repeated it. "One two three four one two three four. When you bring your hands in on beat two, keep some distance between them and never ever cross them—" she demonstrated the cardinal sin, placing her right hand left of her left hand. Then three/ four time is down, out, and up. That's what you need to practice at home, because that's the time signature for the Star-Spangled

Banner. Two/four is the simplest but also the most tiring—at least if you're doing it right. Out, up. Out up out up," she punctuated with fluid motions. "That's what you'll use during parade."

She walked around the piano to the stereo. "Let's run through this together," she said, and when there was a clunking sound on the tape she raised her hands. They all did the same. When the national anthem started, she brought them down, but not before a little upward flourish that signaled the upbeat before the first note. Watching her, Joe remembered seeing a conductor when he was little and thinking he was a magician, summoning and shaping the music with his hands. He thought of Mickey Mouse in *The Sorcerer's Apprentice*, making ocean wave cymbal crashes and shooting-star fanfares. When he gave up his childhood career goal of wizarding, he'd thought that conductors were as close to the real thing as he could get. Of course, that had come with the naiveté that predated *playing* a musical instrument, which was where the real magic was.

Joe was pleased to find he had a knack for conducting. Toni showed them little details and tricks that he picked up quickly. They counted off to set the beat before playing, *one two three four*, but body language was everything. Subtleties helped, like widening one's stance during dramatic, driving parts of the song. Toni held her arms under their hands to bounce off them, and told them to imagine their hands bouncing off a surface while they were conducting.

She told them that overall, there were four things to bear in mind: timing—being on-time was the basis of the whole thing; clarity—not having sloppy, ambiguous beats; emphasis, and expression—reacting to and encouraging the mood of the song.

They went outside. Joe helped Toni carry the stereo out, and Thomas untangled a long extension cord to power it from inside. The parade marching was to be learned core-style, which meant only with their hands, though the selected drum major would have the option of using a baton if he or she chose. Toni walked them through it: calling the band to attention, the whistle for *forward march*, four steps before beginning to beat time to the Sousa, the salute, and finally the *halt* whistle. This was harder, but Joe thought he was at least keeping up. And then, before he knew it, a third of his scheduled training time was over, and he was waiting for the late bus.

Joe felt good. And he wanted to talk about it all to somebody. So it was cruel that his momentary happiness would be snuffed out so quickly. He realized that he had no one to tell how he felt he really had a shot at this—may even have found his talent at long last.

If he was honest with himself, he had no friends. There wasn't anyone who shared his ideas about what was important in the world, who seemed to think that news was worth following and ideals worth fighting for. No one thought like him, enjoyed what he enjoyed, no one understood him. He had never, in the long years from childhood to adolescence to this burgeoning adulthood, found his people. He had a network of acquaintances who liked him well enough, but no one, he thought, who would really care for long if he were to die. Without even establishing that minimal human contact, what was the point?

Chapter 16

Joe endured a month on the edge of a precipice. During math class (of course) he finally decided to kill himself. Both parts of his mind agreed. When it came to emotion, he was in quicksand, which didn't suck him up right away but kept tugging at him as he slogged through it toward a dry ground that never came. There was a constant sense of sorrow, sometimes subtle and in the back of his mind, and sometimes right up front, raw and burning. A fog that numbed everything, and a thickness in his throat that never dissolved.

When it came to logic—what was he living for? There were moments of happiness in his daily routine, it was true—something would make him laugh, or a song would make him smile. But the pain outweighed the joy, and was that any way to live a life? He couldn't live for songs he liked and books he enjoyed.

Nor could he live for his mother. The anguish he would cause her by taking his life was unthinkable, and it tortured him to imagine her in that kind of pain. It's the most terrible thing I can think of, she'd said before, a parent burying a child. Wouldn't suicide make that even worse? Yet, even if it were selfish, Joe didn't know if he could endure his whole life for her sake. Might it get better, if he let the decades of his natural life unroll themselves? Joe wasn't sure anymore, and it seemed to him that the question itself had finally become moot. He'd spent his entire life waiting for it to get better. Had he had a good childhood? He never looked back on it because whenever he did he felt ashamed. He had been *stupid* then, and even as he knew that little kids were *supposed* to be stupid, he couldn't logic away the feeling. Was that some kind of complex? Who cared? He felt pretty sure it could be traced back to his father—*You know better!*—and felt petty even recognizing it. He could lay blame, but he had an idea that the ultimate responsibility for any individual's life lay with the person himself. If he wasn't cut out for living, that was his own weakness.

A diatribe kept running through his head. The thoughts were his, and they tasted bitter because they felt like truth. The early longing for a loving companion, a girlfriend, the greater freedom that adolescence promised. And I'll make more friends at Foothill Middle School. And I'll find people like me in high school. And I'll finally find my place in college. All the while jumping through their damned hoops: learn algebra—okay. Chemistry?—you got it. Anything you feel is important for me to fill my head with and spend precious days of my life learning, even though people admit they don't use these things in real life. And Peter goes to Nathan's house on the weekend but I've got to go thirty miles to my dad's house because that's the way the cookie crumbles, the way the old custody falls. So no wonder I don't have any friends and no wonder I'm shy so I'm my own worst enemy on that front.

He thought of the hundreds of times he had left his dad's house for school determined to never set foot there again, that there was only so much belittling he could take before he had to take a stand. But it never happened. He had told his mother early on that he wanted to switch the arrangement, for her to have full custody over him. But she had almost certainly been right in that they couldn't have won in court against a lawyer. It wasn't as though his father beat him, after all. Then he had thought, more than once, *I'll just refuse to go—Dad can't physically force me to go.* But it never happened. He was a pushover, same as he'd been with Vanessa.

And oh, by the way, he raved in the silent manner of talking he used to use for prayer, *let's give a young boy desperate for meaning the same barrel of lies we've been telling for millennia. Let's tell him that if this world feels hostile to him that's only natural because there's a better world he really belongs in and hey if any of this seems a little weird to you that's okay because there are some things that we just can't comprehend and Proverbs says to lean not on your own understanding and just so you know your asshole dad whom you love anyway is going to Hell if he doesn't accept Jesus as his personal savior but just sayin'.*

Joe feared that when he killed himself the Christians would point out that he'd just left the loving arms of God, so this was why Jesus was so important. Joe might not be happy, but he knew plenty of happy people who weren't religious, and besides that he believed enough in the value of truth to know he'd rather be unhappy and know the truth than cheerfully swallow bullshit. The blue pill or the red one, Neo?

What it all really came down to, when the rage and resentment faded into something more mellow but just as unbearable, was this: Joe King was tired. It was true that he'd lived his whole life *enduring*, just to get to the next plateau, when things would finally get better. But *better* was far from certain, and no, that was no way to live a life.

He had a plan, was turning it over in his head as he got onto a different bus than usual at the end of the day. It was the same bus he could take on Tuesdays to the church for youth group. There was a nature reserve just past Auberry, in New Auberry as it was grandiosely called, although nothing much ever developed there. The road sign just called it Auberry 2.

The reserve was called Squaw Leap, and as Joe recalled it was so named because of an oral tradition about a young Native American man deeply in love with a girl in his tribe. Joe couldn't remember whether the lovely maiden (who would have dark eyes and an irresistible shape, of course) had been killed somehow or simply turned the squaw down, but either way, he had been so distraught in his broken heartedness that he leapt off a cliff to his death.

Joe figured if it worked for the Indian, it should work for him.

The bus pulled away from the curb. Joe watched the leaves on the oak trees, trying to take in every detail. Was he in the last hours of his life? Was he really, after having considered it off and on for years, going to go through with it? He thought so, but there was a little voice in the back of his mind that reserved the right to alter course in response to changing conditions. That voice was a pain in the ass because it would have been really nice to just embrace the end.

He was there in no time. He started the walk down Smalley Road, into the reserve. The last road he'd ever walk, he thought. He couldn't stop thinking things like that. He passed a sign saying, "Property of San Joaquin Valley Nature Conservatory." *The last outfit I'll ever wear—not including the suit for my coffin—and I wasn't even thinking about it when I put it on this morning.* The last how many breaths, how many heartbeats? Would he be alive two hours from then? A half hour?

He was scared but the pain was very real then too, that from which he was trying to escape. Far from feeling relief, Joe was depressed at the desperation of the act—at the grief his family would feel—just his family though, and that was part of the reason he had to do this. He imagined his acquaintances at school when the news broke. It would shock them, some would cry, but they'd get over it quickly enough. He was nobody's best friend, nobody's *close* friend. He would not be missed.

A pressure pushed down on him. It was a wonder he could walk, was not flattened on the ground under the weight of it all. Errant tears rolled down his cheek. He brushed them away. Then he was surprised by real sobs, noises he hadn't emitted since childhood, with snot running down his nose and everything. He walked.

He had his headphones on, but hadn't been paying attention to the songs that shuffled through. Now he did, to a song by the Decemberists. The song was about death, as rock songs often are. It was perversely appropriate.

Go to sleep now, little ugly.
Go to sleep now, you little fool.
Forty winking in the belfry
You'll not feel the drowning.
You'll not feel the drowning.

Forget you once had sweethearts,
They've forgotten you.
Think you not on parents,
They've forgot you too.
Go to sleep now, little ugly
Go to sleep now, little fool.
Forty winking in the belfry
You'll not feel the drowning
You'll not feel the drowning

Hear you now the captain,
Heed his sorrowed cry.
The weight upon your eyelids
Is dimes laid on your eyes.

Joe turned a corner and saw the earth drop away from the pavement up ahead. Beyond it lay the valley below and the tall, smooth top of Table Mountain on the far side. Things were starting to be green and beautiful again. How strange, to die in the season known for bringing life.

Joe approached the edge and looked down. There was a sharp drop of ten or fifteen feet before the earth formed a more level downhill slope. Not much of a cliff. He kicked a chunk of granite into the open space, counted *one-one thou*—before it struck the soft grass and rolled.

He kept walking, looking for a higher place and a longer drop. Nature was oblivious to his pain. Moss bathed in the sun.

He found the most promising place on the end of a jutting stone over a drop. It was a thirty foot drop, he estimated, and that onto soft earth.

Now or never. He turned his back on the edge. He crossed his arms over his chest as though he were already in his coffin. It was the trust fall all over again, but this time he would be trusting the ground to catch his spine or skull just right. Trusting it to kill him, not to leave him hurt and bleeding with broken bones—he didn't want that, not a slow agonizing death, and not an embarrassing discovery and rescue either.

He peeped one more time. The ground looked even closer. It wasn't going to kill him, the Squaw Leap story was bullshit, and he felt ridiculous. This was like a fucking Sierra marching band Salute to Suicide.

He paced off the rock. What now, go home and kill himself there? But he didn't want his mom to find him and there was still the question of how. Pills creeped him out—the idea of swallowing them and then just waiting for it to happen. He found he feared death less than dying. God, if only he had a gun! How quick and uncomplicated that would be!

A petty little thought popped up unbidden in his mind. It was of drum major tryouts, of all things. He thought, and reached an agreement with himself: the auditions were a week after tour. If he was picked to be drum major, he'd stick through senior year. If not, he'd go in the tub and slit T's into his arms, short slashes at the wrist and long cuts down to his elbow.

Joe walked back and caught the last bus from Auberry Elementary School.

Chapter 17

T our wasn't such a bad way to spend the last week of your life. It was Joe's favorite part of the year. One Wednesday in May they all met early in the band room with sleeping bags, suitcases and instruments, loaded up two school buses, and took off.

"This is, for all intents and purposes, your final exam," Mr. Greenberg told them before they left. "You won't receive a grade, just like you won't receive any formal evaluation in life. But you will be tested in all the ways we've prepared for this year—both musically, and when it comes to working as a group and making the right decisions."

Joe sat by Ilse on the bus, on the seat across from Peter and Alyssa, and not far from where Hank sat with his friends. This first day had the longest bus ride of the week, going south of LA all the way to Oceanside. Throughout the ride, papers were passed back to them, which they kept in yellow envelopes. Some gave instructions like *without standing up from your seat, make a list of everyone on your bus*, or *List the activities you'd do if you weren't afraid*, or *until the next stop, do not say the words* I, me, you, the, a, *or* and. Sometimes the papers were little stories, often funny ones with a moral about never undervaluing anyone or a little kindness going a long way.

Finally Joe realized that the smell he hadn't noticed smelling for the last ten minutes or so was the salty air of the coast. He began looking out the window more often (it was easy, Ilse was by the aisle) and soon enough he saw it behind the hills: a blue expanse, stretching on and out, that first glimpse of the ocean that for Joe had always been an important part of any trip to the coast.

Oceanside students waved signs at them as they finally reached their destination. PIZZA, one of the signs proclaimed. McDONALD'S, said another. Joe stuck with Thomas and the others and followed a friendly Oceansider to the nearby pizza joint, a walk of five minutes or so. Much different than Auberry, Joe thought with envy. Before leaving to eat they unloaded all their things from the bus, a small delay that made Joe's pizza all the more transcendent. Their hosts were So-Cal hipsters, and Joe felt more than a little like a bumpkin next to all the punks.

2

Mr. Greenberg addressed their audience with his omnipresent red foam-tipped microphone. "Music," he said, "is a wonderful thing. It is one of life's greatest joys. But music also has a huge capacity to carry a message. This next piece is by an avant-garde composer named Bukvitch, called *In Memorium: Dresden*. The city of Dresden, Germany was one of the cultural centers of the entire world. It contained many museums with priceless art and artifacts, and was a magnet for European bohemians, intellectuals, and artists of all stripes. In World War II, Dresden was never expected to be a target for any military campaign because it had no strategic value at all. There were no Nazi headquarters, barracks, or military presense whatsoever, only a large civilian population.

"The Allied forces bombed it for the devastating blow it would deliver to German morale. But they did not just bomb it; they firebombed it. What this means is that before any actual bombs were dropped, airplanes dropped large quantities of flammable gel all around the city. Only then did they drop the bombs. What occurred was a firestorm. The entire city burned hot enough to create a powerful wind current, so that the fire was self-sustaining. Temperatures reached around 1500 degrees Fahrenheit, and winds 150 miles per hour. Tens of thousands of civilians—including of course, women and children, were killed, but in different ways.

"Many burned to death. Families seeking safety in air raid shelters were cooked. Others were swept like leaves into the air by the extreme winds. The heat and wind created bizarre pressures and vacuums that ripped open people's bodies. They exploded. The city burned for two days. 25 thousand were killed."

The audience was silent. The band played. The first movement of the song was soft and suspenseful. Dresden waited for Yeat's rough beast to come slouching its way. The reeds played their unearthly cycles faster. Joe puckered his lips with the rest of his section and whistled. First high, but steadily descending. Things were beginning to happen. The trumpets played disjointed notes. And Joe, in his desire to captivate the audience, found himself captivated as never before. He saw old men, and women holding babies who would never speak their first word. They looked to the night sky, their Saxon brows troubled. The war had not sent them to the front lines or the gas chambers. The war came to them where they were, and the war killed them, because killing is what war is good at. They heard objects falling, but no booms, not yet, and wondered if there was still time to get to the bomb shelter. Perhaps one German, a young boy or a wizened women, would look out their window and see the splat of jelly and be puzzled, or worse, understand.

The music drifted away from this for a moment to remember Dresden as it was. Sections echoed a beautiful, dignified melody. Joe saw sunshine, students walking across a university square encircled by green. Quartets played in the shopping centers and a painter frowned at the ruffled feathers of a dove. They were making art, making love. Hoping, believing that life could be good, that the world could be saved.

Then a boom, and the lights went out. Flashlights tainted red flashed when the drumbombs sounded.

Boom.

Joe saw, as though he was some impotent angel or the spirit of one already dead, the first homes catch flame. There was a blowing sound. It came from everywhere. The trumpets removed a small curved pipe from their instruments and blew over the ends. The band gave voice to their screams.

"*Hilfe!*"

"*Feur!*"

"*Rauch!*"

"*Hilfe!*"

"*Feursturm!*"

Hilfe struck Joe the most: *help!* He could see the wide-eyed people start to scream, to back into corners and shield their faces in their hands. Everything got louder. The booms began to have no space between them. The brass trilled high, rusty panic. More people screamed. The noise just grew and then it was everyone screaming *Hilfe Hilfe Feursturm* louder and faster all the girls shrieking it and a man was burning he was burning and he stopped dropped and rolled like you're supposed to but the flames stayed on his arms and legs and back and he screamed. Joe felt his own voice pushed beyond and replaced by something high and inhuman. *Rouch rouch rouch feur hilfe* and the mother lived just long enough to see her baby's eyes pop out of his head *hilfe hilfe hilfe HILFE HILFE HILFE*.

And then silence, and one last oboe mourning, and the bombing was over. They were dead and it couldn't have gone on forever so it was over now.

But what kind of a race were they, humans, to commit such evil? And to keep doing it?

Hilfe.
Hilfe.

3

They went to Hollywood. They went to Disneyland. They rode Space Mountain. They rode the bus. On those hours-long rides they discussed the meaning of life with the energy that only the young can master for the subject.

"You're not a hardcore Christian anymore?"

"Nope. Not even softcore."

"That's crazy. Good for you. It's different for someone like me who's never been religious. You don't see too many people change their minds like that."

A meeting of the minds. Joe lost track of who said what; the talk seemed to flow organically from point to counter-point.

"I think the point of life is to be happy."

"So hedonism then."

"Sure, I'd be okay with that."

"But it's not necessarily hedonism. Satisfaction is different than just pleasure. You can be fulfilled by helping people."

"Do we have to help people?"

"No."

"We're all in the same boat."

"If there is no God, that means we find our own purpose."

"Existentialism."

"Ism, ism, ism."

"There is no purpose. We don't need a purpose," said an unapologetic nihilist.

"Maybe *you* don't need a purpose."

"We're all animals. We're smart monkeys. We're programmed to mate and further the species. That's not so bad. I don't know what you'd call that philosophy . . . naturalism?"

"Fuck if I know. Sounds good."

At night they played games on the floors of gyms and churches. They turned the lights out and felt faces in the dark, trying to guess their partner. One night Joe found himself staring at a blonde girl he hardly knew. He went to talk to her, and watched her soft lips as she spoke. Smart monkeys indeed.

When they performed, they played *Pirates of the Caribbean*, and Joe loved that piece. When he played it, he felt every emotion Klaus Badelt had put into it. He even felt the rests and pauses, achingly. The notes had been printed on paper, and he loved the feeling of reanimation when the band breathed them into life. It felt like truth and love. Joe struggled to express these things to Mr. Greenberg after a performance.

"What you felt," Mr. Greenberge told him, "those are the moments musicians live for."

Joe began practicing his conducting to the tune at night.

They talked politics on the bus. They hoped the Democrats would take back Congress, but predicted Schwarzeneggar would stay in Sacramento. An inspirational Einstein quote distributed to the bus sparked a conversation about other famous socialists. Helen Keller and Martin Luther King were mentioned. The general consensus was that socialism wasn't the evil it was made out to be. They were a generation that came of age while the rest of the country was shifting rightward, and they reacted against the excesses of their parents' generation. Even at a hick high school there were intellectuals if you looked in the corners.

Seagulls wheedled on the beach. The ocean's smell pervaded everything. Somewhere on tour Joe decided he wanted to live.

He'd wanted to die because he felt powerless. He was powerless in the way all minors are—his parents' ward. But Joe sent the orders from his brain to the rest of his body. All power expands from that start. No one could truly force him to do anything. Even a gun to the head is only a tool of persuasion. It was believing in powerlessness that brought the sickness.

Still when he looked out the window at the telephone poles all he saw was crosses, and if he didn't blink, blood ran down the outstretched arms of gruesome messiahs there.

Back home, he went to drum major tryouts on Monday. He went to the last concert of the year on Friday.

Chapter 18

"**W**ould Ilse Oliver, Hank Roberts, Joe King and Thomas Gordon please stand up," said Mr. Greenberg.

Joe stood up with the rest of them, he in the trumpet section, they in their own. The songs were over. The awards and recognitions were over. This was the grand finale.

He saw his dad in the audience, wearing jeans and a sweater. It was sort of a relief not to see him in his suit. There was Vanessa's mom and stepdad, near the front. He remembered how they never trusted him. That was okay, they didn't trust anyone. He saw his mother and Tobias. The lights gleamed off Tobias's bald head, and Joe unexpectedly loved him for it.

"The drum major," Mr. Greenberg said while honoring Toni, "is my vital copilot. Without them, I'd be lost.

"This year was the hardest year since I began teaching here to choose next year's drum major. Any one of the four students who came forward would be truly excellent for the job." Warm applause broke out.

Mr. Greenberg handed an envelope to Toni. Joe saw her fingers wrestle, tear, and pull out a paper. Not even she knew what it said before the fact. She stepped to the red microphone.

"Next year's drum major is Joe King."

It took him a second to process his own name. But then people were cheering, clapping hard. The sense of unreality persisted. He walked to Mr. Greenberg and Toni, hugged them. Toni's embrace was warm and feminine, Mr. Greenberg's like that of a family member. The applause was a tangible envelope of good feelings. It announced this moment was his for eternity.

"I'm very proud of you," Ralph King told him afterward. He might always be an asshole, but he said that. That was enough.

Acknowledgements

My huge thanks to everyone who waded through the earliest drafts: Dani, Sarah Melville, Brandon, Ben, Sarah Rittenour, Michelle, Conor, Matt, Laura, Lauren, Sarah Maxwell, Blair, Amanda, Caroline, Molly and Erik. I am so lucky to have such friends.

Works Cited

Caedman's Call. <u>Songs of Worship and Praise</u>. Record.
    City on a Hill, 2000.
The Decemberists. <u>The Crane Wife</u>. Record.
    Capitol/Rough Trade, 2006.
King, Stephen. <u>Wizard and Glass</u>. New York: Grant, 1997.
Thompson, Craig. <u>Blankets</u>. New York:
    Top Shelf Productions, 2003.
Vonnegut, Kurt. <u>Slaughterhouse-Five</u>. New York:
    Delacorte, 1969.